A Fantasy Writer's H...

Rich

2

First published June 2019.

ISBN: 9781097781331

www.richiebilling.com

Acknowledgements

I'd like to thank everybody who chose not to laugh when I told them I wanted to give up my job to write stories. Reading through those dreary first drafts, encouraging improvement and inspiring hope, you've always been there. The journey has been long and tough and without you, I wouldn't have made it this far.

I would also like to thank Mark Vernall who once again has excelled with his artwork. If you find my words of no use, at least you'll have something interesting to look at.

Contents

Part Two: Writing in the Fantasy Genre

Part Three: When The Writing Is Done

A Brief Introduction

They say write the book you want to read. When I first started writing fiction, with nothing but ideas and enthusiasm and an ignorance of the elements of storytelling, this is the book I would have wanted as my guide.

Over the years I've spent countless hours studying the craft of writing and practising and honing that craft. I've learned many lessons, often in the harshest of ways, and the product of those lessons is this book: a guide to everything I've learned about writing, the fantasy genre, and the things that come when the writing is finished, if indeed it ever is.

The aim is to save you the long hours I've spent trawling through textbooks, sitting through lectures, seminars, workshops and scouring the web for every useful little morsel that can be found. It's by no means a complete guide, but it'll set you on the right path.

In the pages that follow you'll find guidance on aspects of writing I find rarely feature in other books, and at times the focus will shift away from the technical elements and consider the philosophies behind writing, ways to help you maintain focus, and methods of battling the demons of doubt that forever loom over our shoulders.

We'll look at the thriving genre of fantasy and the many facets that make it what it is, before turning to the histories of our world that so often inspire fantasy tales.

Lastly, this book will look at the things that come after the story is finished—formatting, peer reviewing, finding publishers—and other things the contemporary writer can do to enhance their careers, such as making and maintaining a website, blogging, and promoting work.

By the end, you'll have a sound foundation upon which to build and the tools to venture out alone with courage and confidence. To help reach that point, all you need is a commitment to work hard and the determination to overcome the challenges ahead.

Let us scribble forth.

Part One:

The Pillars of Storytelling

What Makes You Put A Book Down?

It's here we begin the journey—a critical look at the things that make us grimace and discard a book to the shelves to gather dust for years before donating it to the charity shop. Why, you may ask? As we'll come to see, there's no right way to go about writing, so perhaps a more helpful approach is to look at where it can go wrong.

Sometimes it's hard to pinpoint what we like about a book. More often than not, when we don't like a book we can find the words to say why. I decided to carry out some research into this, and the results, I think, provide a nice structure for the rest of this book.

I wrote to book reviewers and undertook polls on a number of Facebook writing groups: AmWritingFantasy (693 members), Fantasy Writers Support Group (5,447 members), The Phoenix Quill (846 members), and Writing Bad (8,000 members).

The results give some suggestion as to what readers value most in stories, as well as providing an insight into what they dislike. Let's delve deeper.

The book reviewers

A thousand thank you's to the bloggers who kindly responded to my query. In taking the time to get involved you've helped the credibility of this research. This is the question I asked them:

> *"What makes you put a book down and*
> *banish it to the pits of hell?"*

Here are their answers...

Charlotte Annelise

Website: https://charlotteannelise.wordpress.com/
Twitter: @charannelise

What really makes me want to throw a book I'm reading out the window is when the pacing is slow. Books need action to draw the readers in and make them invested in the story. When the plot is so boring that, I cannot even read for longer than a page, that is when I really feel like returning the book to my bookshelf where it will likely collect dust and never be thought of again. I recently DNF'd a book that had a scattered plot without a clear focus. This also attributes to the plot being mind-numbing and difficult to read. While a book's plot does not need to be carved in stone, it helps if it includes interesting plot points that the readers know will be solved later in the story. If all the protagonist is doing is their normal day-to-day activities, it is hard for me to find a reason to keep reading. Thankfully, I rarely find books to be so boring that I want to DNF it, so I think most authors are able to make their stories thrilling enough for me to keep reading.

B.B. Morgan

Website: https://bbmorganblog.wordpress.com/

Twitter: @BBMorgan_W

The number one reason why I stop reading a book is the writing. I can read anything that's well written, be it nonfiction about Nebraska or a YA romantic fantasy. The writing needs to be engaging. I'm not just talking about having A+ grammar and punctuation, I'm talking style. I'll give you the short version (bullet points!) of my turn-offs when it comes to writing: 1) stupid dialogue 2) stage-direction narration 3) boring, repetitive sentence structure 4) purple prose that doesn't go anywhere or adds anything 5) using big words where smaller words would have sufficed and 6) telling, not showing.

Kerry Parsons

Website: https://chataboutbooks.wordpress.com/

Twitter: @bellaboobos11

Thankfully I haven't had to give up on many books. Some are obviously more memorable than others, but I generally enjoy them at the time. Books I haven't got on with tend not to flow well for me. If it's too much like hard work trying to keep track of everything and everyone I will lose interest. I always worry that there's something I'm missing though, especially if it's a book most people have loved. Characters can sometimes be a turn off too. Not necessarily unlikeable characters, because they can be interesting, but characters I just don't gel with at all for whatever reason. If they irritate me I might not care what happens to them and lose interest in their story. Then again, some get under your skin, however irritating, and make their stories all the more compelling. It really does vary. Character and place names which are hard to pronounce can be off-putting too, sometimes. If I find myself not really bothered about reading that next chapter then I know a book isn't working for me and sometimes it's hard to pinpoint why. Life is too short though and my TBR list is way too long to spend time reading something I'm not enjoying. There's always an element of guilt though as I know how much hard work goes into writing, but it would be a boring world if we all loved the same things.

TheGirlOnTheGo

Website: https://wordscantfathom.wordpress.com/
Twitter: @TheGirlOnTheGo8

Books provide me a secret escapade when I really need a break from reality. But that was before. Now, I can't go without a book even for a day. And sleeping with a book by my bedside is a must, it doesn't matter if I don't read, it just has to be there. So when it comes to my biggest pet peeve concerning books, I must admit I really hate a poorly written one, and by that I not only refer to the writing style, but also the various proofreading and editing errors that surface every now and then. That just makes me cringe and I feel like shutting the book for good.

Jason P. Crawford (Beyond the Curtain of Reality)

Website: http://curtainofreality.blogspot.co.uk/ /
http://www.jasonpatrickcrawford.com/home.html
Twitter: @jnewmanwriting

The main thing that makes me banish a book is a clear lack of story flow. This can come in a few forms - if the prose is choppy and ridden with grammar errors, then I can't keep reading; if the writer drops a huge block of exposition in my lap right off the bat, then I'm going to put it down. I wouldn't consider myself a picky reader, but if I can't immerse myself in your story because your errors or style keep me out of it, then I'm not going to give it my time.

The poll results

At 14,986 the sample size was pretty big. I chose the above-listed groups because their memberships tend to be more active. Polls were open for a week. It's hard to give a definite figure on how many people took part—people could vote more than once and Facebook doesn't give much by way of analysis. Voters were allowed to propose their own reasons as well as voting for existing ones. Thirty-five different reasons were put forward in all, some of which overlap.

Reason	Total Votes
Poor/weak characterisation	149
Confusing or unclear plot	134
Too much info-dumping	100
Unedited manuscript	98
Slow plot/nothing to keep you invested	82
Poor grammar/spelling, bad sentence structure	66

Sunshine, rainbows, and evil villains who are evil because they are evil. Oh, and the good guys inevitably win because they're good	41
Annoying or stupid protagonist	40
Poor or weak hook	23
Telling not showing	22
Trite plot	21
You must believe in god/Allah/FSM	19
Romanticised abuse, mental illness, crimes, etc.	17
Lack of plot development	15
Preachiness	14
Don't hurt my hero!	13
A quick dive to the bottom of the cliché barrel	13
Failing to adhere to rules of the world	10
Lack of believability	10
Emotionally empty	7
Not enough description	7
Homophobic	6
Mary Sue/Garry Stu main characters	4
Author biases	4
Slow or boring	3
External interruptions	3
Written like Ernest Hemingway	2
Bland narration	2
Interpreting the Hero's Journey literally	2
Not the ending I wanted	2
Over description	2
Not written like Ernest Hemingway	1
Writing minorities and The Other poorly	1

Characters used as a plot device	1
Unnecessary romance	1

What do the results reveal?

Reading is subjective. One person may laud something another loathes. To quote Kerry Parsons above, "it would be a boring world if we all loved the same things." But a few trends are apparent and they're worth paying attention to.

Strong characters and an engaging plot keep pages turning. What's your favourite book? Was a particular character the main draw? The reason I kept on reading Patrick Rothfuss's *The Name of the Wind* was that I liked Kvothe so much. Here's what one voter had to say:

> *"Plot and characters are everything. If I don't care what happens to the characters and I have no idea what going on because someone is piling on foreshadowing but solving nothing, it's unreadable."*

Too much exposition, i.e. the info dump, is another big problem for readers, it seems. Here's what the voters had to say:

> *"Books traditionally published have a hard time gripping me when there's a lot of info dumping, the exposition is too flowery/unnecessary."*

"Some things, like info dumps or bad sentence structures, usually show themselves on page 1, so if I see a lot of those I will put down a book almost immediately"

An unedited manuscript is another big reason for the reader putting down books. Jason P. Crawford said above: "If the prose is choppy and ridden with grammar errors, then I can't keep reading." But interestingly a lot of voters seemed to suggest forgiveness when it comes to the odd error, provided the story has other strengths, as these comments from voters suggest:

"Give me phenomenal characters and most everything else is forgivable."

"Make the first chapter as perfect as possible so all I see is the wonderful story and characters, then I will be forgiving of errors later."

"I can deal with unedited provided the story is actually still strong."

This is not an excuse to skip or rush editing. It's perhaps the most important aspect of the writing process, yet impatience is understandable. When you've just finished a story all you want to do is share it with the world. But would a painter reveal a half-finished painting?

Above all, these results give us direction. We know what readers value. Let's see how we can satisfy them.

Character

I. Egri's Bone Structure

I've read and heard much about creating characters, learning about them, and making their acquaintance. There's no approach I've found better than that of 'the bone structure', a method set out by playwright Lajos Egri in his book, *The Art of Dramatic Fiction*.

Henrik Ibsen, when discussing his working methods, described how he must 'learn to know' his characters, and how 'painful and slow' this process is. With his wonderfully analytical insights of human nature, Egri has sought to address this.

> "*It is not enough, in your study of a man, to know if he is rude, polite, religious, atheistic moral, degenerate. You must know why. We want to know why man is as he is, why his character is constantly changing, and why it must change whether he wishes it or no.*"

But how can we gain these insights, this deeper understanding that Egri refers to? Why, with the bone structure, of course.

The bone structure is comprised of three parts: **physiology, sociology, and psychology.** They are referred to by Egri as dimensions, and if each dimension of a character is understood, it will make them three dimensional, alive almost.

Physiology consists of a character's sex, age, height and weight, the colour of hair, eyes and skin, their posture, appearance, defects and heredity.

> *"Our physical make-up...influences us endlessly, helping to make us tolerant, defiant, humble, or arrogant. It affects our mental development, serves as a basis for inferiority and superiority complexes."*

As Egri puts it, a hunchback is going to see the world in a completely different light to an Adonis. These physiological factors shape who we are at the basest of levels. To further understand our characters, we must consider their **sociological** factors.

Sociology plays a massive part in shaping who we are. Somebody born and raised in a slum is going to have a different set of reactions to someone born with a silver spoon in their mouth in a sixteen-bedroom mansion. Yet we cannot draw simple assumptions. Other factors ought to be accounted for, such as a person's parentage, and the influence their parents have over them. Likewise, who are their friends, and how do they affect them, and vice-versa? It trickles down to things like the books the person likes to read, the TV shows they enjoy watching, whether or not they're fashion conscious. In exploring these things, we're seeking to understand how society has shaped them.

The product of both physiology and sociology, is **psychology**—the mental state of our characters. According to Egri, the combined influence of the first two 'gives life to ambition, frustration, temperament, attitudes, complexes. Psychology, then, rounds out the three..." So for instance, if we have a character called Bob who possesses a whopper of a nose, this physiological feature, combined with him being teased endlessly by his friends at school—a sociological factor—may leave Bob extremely sensitive when it comes to his nose, such that he grows angry or annoyed whenever it's mentioned and may result in him getting into fights. Alternatively, it may ruin Bob's life, and he becomes awash with a feeling of despondency and resignation. Either way, the physical feature and societal reaction has affected him psychologically.

> "If we understand that these three dimensions can provide the reason for every phase of human conduct, it will be easy for us to write about any character and trace their motivation to its source." Lajos Egri

Egri provides an excellent guide to accompany the theory, and believed that if the below questionnaire was completed, understood and built upon, the writer would be on solid footing to create the living, breathing characters we crave.

Physiology

1. Sex

2. Age

3. Height and weight

4. Colour of hair, eyes, skin

5. Posture

6. Appearance: good looking, over or underweight, clean, neat, pleasant, untidy, shape and size of features

7. Defects: deformities, birthmarks, diseases

8. Heredity

Sociology

1. Class: working, middle, ruling, bourgeoisie

2. Occupation: type of work, hours, income attitude toward work, suitability of job

3. Education: past schools, universities, favourite and weakest subjects, grades

4. Home life: parents still alive, are they divorced, do they have any bad habits or vices, any siblings? What about the character's own marital status? Any children?

5. Religion

6. Nationality

7. Place in community

8. Political affiliations

9. Hobbies and interests

Psychology

1. Sex life, moral standards

2. Personal premise, ambition

3. Frustrations, chief disappointments

4. Temperament

5. Attitude toward life

6. Complexes: obsessions, inhibitions, superstitions

7. Extrovert, introvert, ambivert

8. Abilities: talents, languages

9. Qualities: imagination, judgement, taste

10. IQ

Depending on the character and their background, different factors may have more sway on who they are and how they think and feel. For instance, a lack of education, of supervision, and the constant presence of poverty and hunger will have a more lasting impact on a particular character. As a result, sociological factors have had a determining factor over the other two.

So the bone structure gives us a foundation. How can we build upon it?

II. Playing God: Tools for Crafting Characters

It's not an easy skill to come up with interesting and compelling characters. As we know, a weak character can lead to a reader shelving a book. This chapter first considers the ingredients which make for interesting characters before exploring some useful tools to help you craft your own.

What makes a character interesting?

So what ingredients should our character broth have? Here are some ideas:

- A character with **conflicted morals**, such as those forced to choose between right or wrong or the lesser of two evils.
- A character that **can do something that no one else can**. Only Frodo with his untainted soul can take the ring to Mordor. Only Daenerys Targaryen can withstand raging flames.
- A character that is **out of their depth**. Prince Yarvi in Joe Abercrombie's *Half a King* admits himself he is the least able person to be King, but try he must.
- **Relationships with others**. Could the character be part of a gang of close friends, like in James Barclay's series *The Chronicles of The Raven*? Or is the character in love with

someone who they cannot be with, or long to be with, like Kvothe and Denna in Patrick Rothfuss's *The Name of the Wind?*

- **A character that reminds us of ourselves**. This is a good way to create empathy, a very important ingredient in making a character likeable, something we'll explore in more detail. The character may do something that the reader has always wanted to do, but is unable. That's the beauty of fiction—possibility.

- A character that's **proactive**, something we'll discuss below.

- A character that has **imperfections**. Not only do imperfections enable the reader to connect empathetically with the character, but they also add a whole layer of conflict for that individual. Think of the different challenges experienced by Tyrion Lannister. Mental challenges could be involved too, like depression or a lack of confidence.

- **Humour**. We naturally like people who entertain us. The Raven in Barclay's books forever joke with each other. Humour isn't restricted to just dialogue. Incidents such as Laurel and Hardy-esque accidents and facial expressions, body language and the like can all have a likeable effect.

This list is by no means exhaustive, but it gives us a bit of an idea of what helps to make a character interesting. Now let's look at how we can put it to use.

Tools for Crafting Characters

Sliding Scales

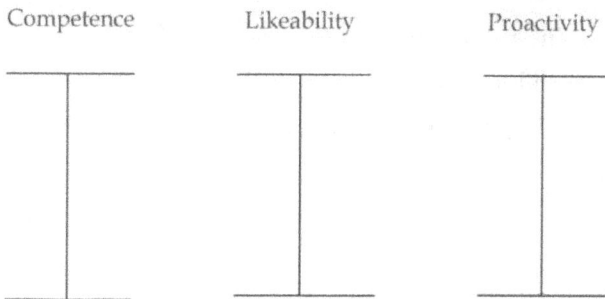

One way to help achieve and measure the effects a character has on a reader is to use sliding scales. This is a technique taught by Brandon Sanderson in his online lectures (all available on Youtube for free. Well worth checking out.)

Brandon Sanderson is of the view that we can strip each character back to three core features, measurable on sliding scales. These scales are **competence**, **likeability**, and **proactivity**. Each scale is very much linked with the other.

Sliding Scales

| Competence | Likeability | Proactivity |

Likeability

In the crafting of your character, it's up to you how likeable you want them to be. Ideally, protagonists should be likeable, but then again we have our anti-heroes like *Breaking Bad's* Walter White.

Antagonists ought to be unlikeable, like Joffrey Baratheon, but again you could employ a likeable bad guy to blur the lines.

How can you manipulate this likeability scale? A good place to start is to think of traits we associate with people we like. They could be kind-hearted, selfless, funny, helpful, considerate of others. An all-round saint. Translating this into words isn't always easy. An effective way is to demonstrate them through actions—*show* the character risking life and limb to save a worm from being trampled on. Another effective way is to have other characters talk about them in positive ways. When we hear people talking about others they know, it's a suggestion of the impression they've left on them. Their likeable or unlikeable actions have made such an impact they feel compelled to tell others about them. Great deeds and heroic acts get people talking, and the stories they tell help to form our perception of who that person is.

How then can you make a character unlikeable? It's said if you want a reader to dislike a character have them kick a dog, or worse, kill it. It's not possible to put a dog in every one of your stories, but this example shows us the sorts of behaviour that provoke negative reactions in readers. Think about immoral actions: lies, deceit, treachery, murder—all those traits we generally dislike in others.

Proactivity

Readers naturally like characters that progress the story, that try their best no matter the odds. Frodo was hell-bent on taking the One Ring to Mordor, regardless of the multitude of obstacles in his path. Richard from Terry Goodkind's *Wizards First Rule*, was utterly determined to help and protect his friends from the evil of Darken Rahl, and constantly strived to complete this objective.

Positivity ties into proactivity. In life, we generally like people who are positive, people who do not complain and make the best of what they've got. A character who is positive tends to be someone who does their very best to get things done.

A reluctant character, riddled with fear, or someone who's content with their lot, would fall low on the proactivity scale. They will not stray far from their comfort zone, will not inspire others to take action. Such characters may, on the face, appear boring, but they have terrific scope for development. How would such a character fare if they were shoved out of that comfort zone? We'll come to character growth shortly.

So what can you do to make a character proactive?

- Give them dreams or aspirations.
- They may have an oath to keep, a promise to fulfil.
- A character may have been forced into a difficult situation, one they must get out of, such as being enslaved or kidnapped.
- A character may have a longing to explore, to break free, to change the life they currently live.

These are but a few; there are many more. See what you can come up with.

Competence

Most characters tend to have some degree of competency in one or more ways. There are, of course, the hapless village idiots that can't do anything right, but in the main, people are generally good at something. The same can apply to characters. You may have a character who's particularly good at smithing, like Gendry from *Game of Thrones*, or someone like Legolas who can shoot the wings of a bee with a bow and arrow from nine miles away. On the top end of the competency scale, we have our superhero legends, like David Gemmell's Druss or Aragorn from *Lord of the Rings*, who single-handedly defeat armies.

A character defined as highly competent tends to be likeable. Why? We enjoy seeing masters or experts going about their business. Over twenty movies in and people still aren't bored of James Bond saving the world, massacring henchmen and blowing shit up. Who doesn't love watching Liam Neeson destroy half of Paris in *Taken*, Gimli battling hordes of orcs or Pug from the *Riftwar Cycle* destroying a planet?

Highly competent characters don't always have to be likeable, though. Take Darth Vader, one of the most powerful Jedi's in the universe yet still a bit of a dick. Most villains tend to be competent at what they do, and indeed the more competent the villain, the greater the threat is to our beloved heroes. How could they possibly defeat such an evil and powerful bastard? Villains have their own chapter, coming up soon.

It's worth remembering that you don't have to limit yourself to these three scales. You could go into more specific detail. If you're a fan of computer games, you could approach it like picking your character's attributes in the likes of *The Elder Scrolls* or *Fallout*.

And remember, just because you set each scale at a certain level doesn't mean it has to stay that way. In fact, one of the most satisfying things in a story is to see the development and growth of characters.

Monologues

A very handy exercise when developing characters is to write a monologue. A monologue is, in essence, a stream of thought noting everything that pops into your mind about a character: names, appearance, likes, dislikes, relationships, history, hobbies, interests, abilities ... the list could go on.

Most of this information may never be used in the story, but in discovering it you grow to know that character as you know yourself. When they're faced with a conflicting or difficult situation in your story, you know exactly how they will act, what they would say, making for more believable characters.

A few final things

I recommend dipping your nose into the book *The First Five Pages* by Noah Lukeman. Lukeman is one of the best literary agents in the industry. He provides useful insights into things to avoid as well as providing solutions and exercises. In it he sets out a few things he recommends avoiding when crafting a character. It should be borne in mind that this is just advice, and good advice too, but if you think going against it benefits your story, then do it.

- Don't jump head first into the story without taking the time to establish the characters.
- Avoid cliché characters, like the Russian spy or the alcoholic policeman.
- Don't introduce too many characters at once. The reader's mind will boggle.
- Make it clear who the protagonist is.
- Make sure characters are relevant, even those on the periphery. If they're not needed it uses up the reader's energy.
- Be creative with character description. A unique description can enhance a story.

III. The Wheels of Change

Everything in this world of ours changes. Mountains crumble into the sea. Islands disappear. Forests become icecaps. Change is eternal. It is one of life's only constants. For some of us, we welcome it, embrace it. Others resist.

Think of ourselves. Most of us want some kind of change in our lives. We want to better our standing, get a job we enjoy more, earn more money, buy more stuff. Think back to the past, to your school years. How many of those best friends are you still in contact with now, and I bet you were inseparable with a few? What would be a thought that would enter your mind when debating whether or not to reach out to them now? *Things aren't the same as they used to be.*

We do not live static existences. Sometimes we change through choice, and other times it is thrust upon us. Even the most ritualistic individuals experience some kind of change that alters their lives in stressful and conflicting ways. The closure of a local pub can cause great distress for the old patrons. What else have they to do with the long and lonely hours of the day? Where else have they to go? It seems mighty trivial, but trust me, I've run a pub. Some people shape their lives around routine, and when what may seem a trivial change occurs, the ripples knock off course everything else in their life.

Change can be good or it can be bad. Often in fiction, we're faced with negative changes, changes that create conflict in the lives of our characters. It's through reacting to these conflicts our characters grow, at times by making the right move and resolving the conflict, or the wrong move and making things worse.

Many fantasy stories involve characters from humble beginnings that, as a result of decisions both voluntarily and involuntarily, go on to achieve greatness. Pug in Raymond Feist's *Riftwar Cycle*, Kvothe in Patrick Rothfuss's *The Name of the Wind*, Frodo and Sam in *The Lord of the Rings*, to name but a few.

By this point, I may hopefully have convinced you in the constant and capricious nature of change. You may now be wondering how it relates to creating characters?

> *"There is only one realm in which characters defy natural laws and remain the same—the realm of bad writing. And it is the fixed nature of the characters that make the writing bad."*
> Lajos Egri.

Characters may go on a physical journey, but often the greatest one of all is the one they go on within themselves, the change they go through as they overcome trials and tribulations, heartbreak and despair.

Let's take a look at what we can do to get that wheel of change spinning.

The decision

Characters can be motivated to act by any number of influences and pressures. Let's take a gambler who's fallen into debt with an unsavoury chap. This moneylender has beaten him for the money, and now is threatening to hurt his family. He is afraid. He's not much of a fighter, nor is he overly aggressive. But he cares deeply for his family. These conflicting pressures force him to make a decision: fight back or flee?

What can influence a decision?

Innumerable factors can influence even the most trivial of decisions, yet so often they fall under the umbrellas of the physiological, the sociological and the psychological—indeed, the very make-up of our characters.

Who we are, what we believe, how we were raised etc. influence what decisions we make and that, in turn, can lead us down paths of change. According to Egri, it's knowing in detail these characteristics that help us determine whether a character has made the choice most consistent with who they are. Or as Egri put it: 'Only in bad writing does a man change without regard to his characteristics.'

Charting growth

There's a nifty tool to help plot character growth, a development line of sorts, known as **'the everyman and the superman.'**

The 'everyman' is the average Joe. The person content with their lot, until life throws a twist, perhaps forcing them on a path they never intended. That path, and the obstacles they must overcome along it, leads them to change and develop as individuals, maybe learning things about themselves they never knew, realising their potential, or gaining new skills to help them become 'supermen' or 'superwomen'.

Generally, a story involving a rounded 'superman' tends to involve a highly competent character saving the world. There isn't much room for character growth because they're already the best at everything, ever. Take James Bond, for example. He's forever foiling plots to destroy the world and nobody ever doubts that he's going to succeed.

Supermen, however, can fall like redwoods, and this is an interesting approach you can take to shake things up. How can that once great character regain their greatness?

The Everyman and the Superman

The decline

A superman can descend into nothingness, or the average person could fall into decline, like Frodo in LOTR as he is corrupted by the ring.

Superman

The superman is the person we want to be. Readers connect with competent characters.

A lot of stories involve every day people growing into superheroes.

Everyman

This is the person we are. Readers can relate to this type of character.

IV. Making Characters Likeable

We do, of course, want our heroes to be likeable. We want to create characters so vivid our readers almost feel them alive, characters whom readers think about as they go about their day. We all have a favourite character, one that stands out amongst the crowd and, as writers, it's our job to create them. Luckily, tools and techniques exist to do this, some of which we've touched upon. Now we're going to look at it in more detail, as well as a technique I feel warranted its own chapter.

Empathy

It's often said that readers engage with empathetic characters, individuals we can relate to in some way, that feel the same feelings we do, that endure the same conflicts and are faced with similar dilemmas. We naturally like to see how other people fare with these challenges, to see how they overcome them. It can inspire and empower us to tackle them ourselves.

By way of example, I'm a massive fan of TV presenter and angler, Jeremy Wade (*River Monsters*). The man is without fear and utterly determined in his pursuits, so much so that I can't help but feel inspired by him. Think of someone you admire, and ask why you do so. How can you transfer those traits to your characters? Do you share something in common with them? Do they possess a trait you wish to have or develop? Do they impress us with a skill or talent (swordsman, archer, singers, footballers etc.)? Have they conquered a fear that we hold ourselves?

The secret snapshot technique

To really open empathy's door for your characters, a technique exists known as the secret snapshot. It's a way of discovering and revealing the deepest, darkest aspects of your characters, those that will marry the reader to your character and their cause. One that exposes the vulnerabilities of your character, giving them an emotional and empathetic edge sharp enough to stir the emotions of your readers. The theory is simple, the practice is more challenging.

The secret snapshot technique was used by master editor Sol Stein in his teaching days. Firstly, he asked his students to think of a truly private memory, a secret most guarded, something they try to forget altogether. It has to be a memory so secretive, that if a snapshot (or photo) of it existed it would be locked away and hidden from the world.

"Some writers squirm through the process, shifting uncomfortably in their seats. That's a good sign." Sol Stein.

To help, I'll give my own example. I have a vivid recollection of the day my mum and dad told me they were splitting up. I was about eleven. I remember crying about not being able to go to football training any more, which my dad took me to each day after school. Looking back, what I was really upset about was the fact that my life was never going to be the same again.

When you've come up with your example, ask yourself whether this is something you'd lock in a box and bury deep in the woods. If yes, think of another. You want to reach deep into your emotional memories to find those most personal.

"The best fiction reveals the hidden things we usually don't want to talk about." Sol Stein.

The bravest writing someone can do is to explore the recesses in which the secret snapshots of their friends, enemies, and themselves are stored.

I think what this nifty tool teaches us above all is the need to really open up the character to the reader. It's the job of the writer to completely expose a character. It can be tough to do, not technically, but emotionally. From experience, I always find a part of me in every character I create, even tiny things. When you find yourself exploring the core emotions of a character you can find yourself writing about things personal to you. Things you maybe don't wish to share. Feel afraid of. That can only ever be a good thing, if not at least for therapeutic reasons. For your writing, it adds genuine emotion and experience.

V. The Bad Guys

"Anyone who opposes a pivotal character necessarily becomes
the opponent or antagonist. The antagonist is the one who holds back
the ruthlessly onrushing protagonist. He is the one against whom the
ruthless character exerts all his strength, all his cunning, all the
resources of his inventive power."

Lajos Egri, *The Art of Dramatic Writing*

The antagonists in the stories we love so much are often just as memorable as the heroes, if not more so. Perhaps one of the most iconic bad guys is Darth Vader. Near enough everybody recognises the sound of that heavy breath and the shape of that helmet. But other than looking and sounding the part, there's much more to Vader that draws us to him, namely the conflicts riddling his mind and soul.

No bad guy is the same, but there are a number of common features that they share, and it's these different features that help to shape what kind of bad guy you want to create. In this chapter, we'll look at three of the more common types of villain, but first, let's consider the make-up of an antagonist.

The make-up of the villain

When we look to the more memorable villains, it's often the case that they are highly competent—at leading, fighting, influencing, using magic, or possessing great size and strength. When we know two enemies are due to clash, but one is mightier and larger than the other, we wonder how on earth the protagonist will overcome the odds and win. And this creates tension. There seems to be one accepted practice when it comes to this—that the antagonist should be at least equal in might to the protagonist, if not more powerful. As Lajos Egri said, "A fight is interesting only if the fighters are matched." I agree with Egri, but I also believe that putting our heroes up against it leads to great storytelling too. Take the Ride of the Rohirrim chapter in Tolkien's *The Return of the King*, for instance.

To really give the villain an edge, it helps to make them highly motivated in the pursuit of their goals. Motivated to the point of relentlessness. Let's look at the example of Sauron. He yearns for the return of the One Ring. He sends out his dark riders and his eye forever scours Middle Earth. He is motivated beyond all else to find it. The same can be said for the White Walkers from *A Song of Ice and Fire* and their desire to bring about the Long Night.

Villains, in general, believe wholeheartedly that their cause is the right one, and the cause of the protagonist is the antithesis to that belief, in their eyes evil, and must be stopped at all costs. In this sense, the protagonist and antagonist share something in common—their unfaltering belief that the other is wrong.

Understanding your villain

There's been a backlash of late against villains of pure evil, the classic, archetypal 'bad guy'. People argue that they're too one dimensional; evil for evil's sake. It seems to have sparked a trend toward the bad guys who blur the lines, who have a foot in both camps. Anti-heroes. This doesn't relegate our classic villains to obsoletion, though. But there is a point to take away from it: that the bad guys need to be more than just props for the story, that they, in fact, have compelling stories of their own.

A part of reading involves exploring new perspectives, experiencing things we could never do, or to feel emotions we're unaccustomed to. We castigate a thief for stealing food, yet when we see the story through their eyes, we learn that he is thieving to feed his starving family. Is he as evil as we thought?

A good starting point when creating an antagonist is to ask questions. The answers will help determine where on the spectrum of evil they lie. Questions could include:

- Do they regularly carry out evil acts, or is this their first time?
- Have they thought about doing it before, or is it instinctive or reactive?
- What are the circumstances that led to their current path of evil?
- What in their past could have shaped them into what they are today?
- Do they garner pleasure or satisfaction from being evil, i.e. sadistic?
- Is this something they've recently discovered?
- How do they justify their actions to themselves or to others?
- What is their underlying motive?
- What do they seek to achieve?

Who's right and who's wrong?

One thing worth considering when crafting a villain is their motivation. Our own lives are dictated by the things we are motivated to do. If you can't be arsed going for a jog, then you're not going to do it. If you're determined and motivated to lose weight, then chances are you'll stick on your shorts despite the lashing rain. Motives drive people, and the same goes for characters.

Motive alone does not suffice, though. To unlock that motivation we must believe and have faith. A person must believe that jog in the pissing rain will help them achieve their goal. The same applies to our villains. They have faith in what they are doing because they believe wholeheartedly it is the right thing to do, even if it involves killing people. From their perspective, they're dead right. Everyone else is wrong. Who cares what they think? It's a megalomaniacal stance and a pretty destructive one at that.

So, let's take a look at a few different types of villain.

Villains of pure evil

When designing a truly evil villain, bad behaviour alone is insufficient to characterise. More must be shown to convince the reader the antagonist is truly evil. Are they corrupted to their core? Are they sadists, deriving pleasure from inflicting pain? Let's look at some examples.

Gollum – always seeking to foil Frodo's plans and reclaim the One Ring for himself. His hatred for the "filthy hobbitses" runs deep. Gollum has been corrupted, his nature fundamentally changed.

Sauron – an example of a character of pure evil. Little is revealed about Sauron's true motives beyond his desire to annihilate the world of men. He is unwavering in his efforts—indeed the eye is always watching—and similarly, he commands an army which also seems to be hell-bent on achieving the same end. Conflicted orcs and goblins are few and far between in Middle Earth, it seems.

Sol Stein says in his book, *Stein on Writing*, that it should be extremely difficult for a villain of pure evil to be re-educated or re-conditioned into a nicer person. Frodo tried that with Gollum and lost a few fingers for his efforts—he still managed to finish Bilbo's book, though.

So how can you characterise such utter bastards?

- **Physical mannerisms.** Think of creepy, involuntary habits such as a twitching eye; pulling hairs out of their eyebrows, moustache or beard; earlobe tugging or lip chewing. Habitual mannerisms seem to work best—the repetitive nature can grate on readers, which is handy if you're trying to create an unlikeable fellow.
- **Competency and an unfaltering determination to succeed.** In *Lord of the Rings*, Sauron's eye is forever seeking, the Ring Wraith's forever hunting. They are effective and efficient, forever on their tail, waiting to prey upon the slightest

mistake. All this creates conflict and jeopardy, things your reader will love.

- **Ask yourself how your antagonist behaves toward people he's never met before.** Some villains come across as pleasant and affable. Gustavo Fring from *Breaking Bad* is a good example of such a villain. He makes donations to charities and has a good relationship with the D.E.A., the very people trying to catch him. Under the surface, he's a ruthless criminal. We can look to real-life nutcases too. Jimmy Saville for example, a once loved children's entertainer and TV presenter, turned out to be a serial paedophile. He gave millions to charity, even helped set up a children's hospital. Talk about blurring the lines.

- You could go the opposite way and have an antagonist who's discourteous, arrogant, or sadistic. Recently I was watching Black Beauty with my grandmother and found myself on the edge of my seat in a mild fury as the Squire lashed at Beauty with his whip. Remember that tip from the previous chapter? If you want the reader to dislike a character, have them kick a dog. Well, it works.

- **Does your antagonist do something frequently that others do occasionally?** Sol Stein gives the examples of a character blowing their nose every few minutes despite not being sick, a forehead slick with sweat when the temperature is cool, persistent coughing or clearing of the throat, or bobbing a leg when sat down cross-legged. All of these things suggest something about the character, about who they really are. It helps them stand out, makes us feel that something isn't quite right.

Examples are useful. Let's look at one from Terry Goodkind's bestseller, *Wizard's First Rule*. For the first 250 or so pages we're merely told about the antagonist, Darken Rahl. And then in chapter nineteen, we see him first hand.

"White roses, replaced every morning without fail for the last three decades, filled each of the fifty-seven gold vases set in the wall beneath each of the fifty-seven torches that represented each year in the life of the deceased. A large staff saw to it that no torch was allowed to go spent for longer than a few moments, and that rose petals were not allowed to rest long upon the floor. The staff were attentive and devoted to their tasks. Failure to be so resulted in an immediate beheading.

Staff positions were filled from the surrounding D'Haran countryside. Being a member of the crypt staff was an honour, by law. The honour brought with it the promise of a quick death if an execution was in order. A slow death in D'Hara was greatly feared, and common. New recruits, for fear they would speak ill of the dead king while in the crypt, had their tongues cut out."

These are just the first two paragraphs of the chapter, and from them, we glean much about Darken Rahl without him even being mentioned. What kind of person would employ such a large workforce just to maintain torches and flowers? What kind of person would kill those workers for the merest of blunders? And then in the second paragraph, we see how serving Rahl is deemed an honour, but only by law. An oppressive stance by whoever enacted that law. And lastly, what kind of influence must a person have on others to compel them to cut out their own tongues for fear of speaking ill of the dead king? Before we even see Rahl, we know what he's like.

The doubtful villain

The classic bad guy archetype has been cleverly adapted over the years. We know one of the main complaints about the evil for evil's sake villain is their lack of conflict. Orcs hate humans. End of. What I've often wondered is whether any of those orcs felt differently. What if they came to see a different perspective, one that made them question their ways and potentially change their course? But how can they break free of that life, the only one they have ever known? Where would they go? What would they do? We choose the easiest path, often the one we know. Sometimes the right way to go is the more difficult route. Herein lies the conflict.

Let's look at an example courtesy of Adrian Tchaikovsky. In his novel *Empire in Black and Gold*, the main antagonist begins to doubt himself and the actions of the empire he's served devoutly his whole life. We're left wondering what he will do—will a man who prides himself on loyalty commit an act of betrayal? The conflict blurs the lines between good and evil and makes us wonder whether, in fact, they are truly evil as we believed.

It can be argued that Jaime Lannister in *A Song of Ice and Fire* is a doubtful bad guy too. One of the first acts we see him do is shove Bran Stark out of the top window of a tower. He is selfish, arrogant, heartless. Yet, at times he seems to be a man of reason, a good guy.

George R.R. Martin is a master at creating characters who sit on the fence of good and evil. Another example from his stories is the Hound. A man who kills Arya's friend and a whole host of other people, yet by the end he finds himself fighting on the frontline for the forces of good.

I like this kind of villain. For me, they epitomise hope. Hope that even fervently evil people can change for the better.

Things have gotten out of hand

There's a growing trend toward the complicated bad guy. The folks that have lived good and innocent lives, only to be corrupted. Why is this the case? One possible explanation is conflict. As we'll come to see when we look at plotting, readers love conflict. Conflict propels stories.

A conflicted bad guy can make for an interesting character. We want to see if they'll go through with the murder, how they'll react when they see blood pouring from wounds. Once upon this evil path, to maintain their status as the central antagonist, it makes sense for them not to deviate. Indeed, Sol Stein advises them to fall deeper into their corrupted ways. Whether voluntarily or involuntarily is up to you.

Plot

I. What's The Plot?

Plot and character go hand in hand. To find a plot true to our characters, we must first understand them, so that when they're faced with conflicts and obstacles we'll know how they'll react. And it's those reactions that help shape the plot.

It's in plotting our character's paths that we truly come to know them. We test their mettle and resolve, push them to their absolute limits. It's in moments such as these we discover what our creations are truly made of. In this chapter, we'll at some techniques you can employ to help map out the hellish journeys your characters could embark upon.

Definitions

Let's get a couple of definitions out of the way before we dive deeper.

> *Story — is a sequence of events. This happened, then that happened ...*

Plot – encapsulates the sequence of events, plus character motivations. A plot develops out of conflicts which affect the characters. An example of a story would involve a man dying, followed by his wife. A plot would involve the death of a man, followed by his wife, only her death is the result of a broken heart.

Character motivation

What the protagonist needs or chooses to do has to matter. For example, a woman's daughter is kidnapped and she has just two days to raise a million pound to pay the ransom. Frodo must take the One Ring to Mordor or risk the destruction of everyone and everything he holds dear. Richard must defeat Darken Rahl—not only is it his task as Seeker, but he must avenge the death of his father.

A strong motive will help that character overcome the obstacles before them. It will give them the courage to defeat a Balrog or face down an entire army. It's the writers' job to test that motivation as much as possible. Ask what you can do to make things even worse for your characters. Send them to the pits of hell and back. Strip them of all their abilities, their confidence.

It's said the focus of the earlier chapters in a novel or story ought to be on characters. If we're to care about the people in the car when it crashes, we need to know about them first. By this I mean before you can start making the lives of your characters a living hell, the reader needs to get to know them, otherwise, they may struggle to care what happens to them.

Character imperfections

If you're seeking to introduce another layer of conflict to your story, something to consider is giving your protagonist an imperfection of some kind. Some people call them flaws but I think that's misleading and disingenuous to the character. Let's explain this one with an example.

Tyrion Lannister. He's a dwarf and fuck me doesn't he know it. His own family, one of the richest and most powerful in all of Westeros, barely tolerate him. Most people in the realm mock him for being half a man. His dwarfism creates a whole layer of conflict in his life, such that it affects how he thinks and acts. It brings with it a unique set of challenges that he must overcome and enriches the tale with a unique perspective. Other writers like Joe Abercrombie have experimented with similar things, such as with Yarvi in his novel *Half a King.* Remember the physiological aspect of the bone structure?

Something I've been experimenting with, and indeed is very relevant in contemporary life, are mental challenges, such as depression, anxiety, and low self-esteem. How could you feature those in your stories?

This isn't to say every character must have an imperfection. There are the supermen we know and love, like David Gemmell's Druss the Legend. But it can be tricky to empathise with perfect characters, for nobody is perfect. Everyone has their failings. You could probably list mine on two sides of A4. We love people regardless. Indeed, their imperfections can be the thing that makes us love them above all else.

Promises

Prolific novelist and all round good guy, Brandon Sanderson, offers an interesting bit of advice when it comes to structuring plots, and that's about making the right kind of promises to you reader.

He's of the view that early on in the story, promises must be made to the reader about what is to come. Novels can be weighty beasts—a significant time commitment. When you sit down to read a gritty thriller and get a couple of hundred pages in, the last thing you want is for the villain to whip out a wand and start turning everyone into potpourri. The reader will feel cheated, annoyed and angry.

So how can this be done? One way is through prologues. There's a fair amount of debate as to the usefulness of prologues. If done well, they can really enhance a story. If done badly you've lost your reader before the story even gets going.

One trap in way of the writers' path is to use a prologue as an opportunity to info dump and world-build. There's a good chance using too many names of people, places or concepts is going to send a reader to sleep. World-building will be discussed in its own chapter, but in short, the most successful and popular technique is to tease details of the world into the story—the odd reference here or there, especially in the first few chapters. Show the tip of the iceberg.

One prologue that's stuck in my mind is from *A Game of Thrones*. Gripping, intriguing, action-packed. Very little magic or supernatural incidents occur in the subsequent chapters, and indeed throughout much of the Song of Ice and Fire books until dragons hatch and white walkers begin their long hike to the wall. Without that prologue, it may be assumed that magic does not exist at all in this world.

Similarly, in Sanderson's book, *Mistborn*, the prologue features Kelsier single-handedly destroying a slave plantation. While you don't know how he did it, we know such a thing is possible.

The prologue in Indiana Jones and the Raiders of the Lost Ark provides another helpful example. We're introduced to this competent character navigating his way through an ancient ruin to recover a treasure. He evades traps and pitfalls, gets what he wants, but at the very end drops the treasure. An exciting opening with promises made about the character—that he's competent but has failings, and immediately we want to know more.

Progress

I find nothing more frustrating than a static story. Don't introduce me to a character and have them do nothing for paragraphs or pages. I know I'm not alone.

In his creative writing lectures, Brandon Sanderson explains the importance of making the reader feel like they are making progress with the story, that they are going somewhere—exploring ancient ruins or vibrant cities, witnessing great battles and experiencing intimate moments in characters' lives.

It doesn't stop at places or adventures, though. A reader must see the characters taking steps to achieve their goals, and often those steps involve the obstacles we as writers throw in their path. If for three chapters the protagonist is just sailing to some faraway land, the reader will end up wanting the ship to sink. What twists could be added? Could they encounter a sea monster, a pirate ship, a deadly storm?

II. Plotting Devices

Devising a plot isn't always a straightforward task, and if there's a lot going on, things can get out of hand. In this chapter we'll look at a few helpful plotting devices. Each one provides a different method of mapping out your story. If one doesn't work for you, another might. Remember, there's no right way of doing things. Just lots of different ways to get to the end.

The bracketing method

If there's a lot going on in your story, with several central characters, it can be tricky to keep track of everything that's going on. George R.R. Martin even admits to losing track and relies on the help of a few *GOT* fanatics to spot any contradictions. To be fair, he has about forty main characters and a small army of supporting characters too.

So how does the bracketing method work?

When a plot or sub-plot begins a bracket is opened. Then as it resolves, the bracket is closed. Let's look at an example:

The Bracketing Method

Introduction. Readers meet characters. Conflicts begin.

Questions arise. Conflicts deepen. Obstacles introduced.

Here is where the main bulk of the story takes place. Sub plots begin to develop.

The twist. Conflicts intensify. Perhaps some character deaths.

The questions that arose at the beginning are answered. Some conflicts resolved.

Conclusion. Protaganist/s ought to have achieved what they set out to do.

The three-act format

This technique is more common in the film industry, yet its foundation in storytelling is sound and its method applicable across the board. This is my personal favourite. It's a simple, easy tool which helps to break down a story. The graphic below describes it:

Three Act Format

Introduction	Confrontation	Resolution
Here the charcaters are introduced, setting is established, the tone is set, promises are made. The first few chapters should focus on the characters, rather than worldbuilding.	This is the biggest part of the story. The prospects of the protagnist turn sour. Conflicts intensify.	The satisfying conclusion. Promises come to fruition. Conflicts are resolved. It is the shortest part of the story.
In between introduction and confrontation we have the crisis point – the conflict. The protagonist is forced into a plot. Things will never be the same for them again. They could be forced on a quest or decide that they must act on something. Ask yourself what is the character trying to accomplish. Their goals and aims must be set out.		In between confrontation and resolution is the lowest point. Do or die time. As an example, in LOTR: Return of the King, the armies of Mordor amass at Minas Tirith and begin the siege. All looks to be lost. Then the horn of Rohan sounds in the distance.

Sanderson's plotting technique

The font of knowledge himself has his own plotting device. He begins by building a list of promises or events that could take place in a story. So for example, if we looked at Star Wars, the key events or promises there:

- Destroying the Empire;
- Defeating an all-powerful Sith Lord (the Emperor);
- A character from humble beginnings learning the ways of the Force;
- Restoring light amongst the universe.

The next step is to ask how can these be achieved. Each point must progress the story toward a conclusion, with interesting conflicts and red herrings along the way. "One simply does not walk to Mordor," as we all know. Thinking of the likes of relationships, mysteries, journeys and character imperfections can all help.

Sub-plots

If your story is following one particular path, with little to break it up, a subplot can provide nice variation. Too many sub-plots, however, can confuse a reader. Sub-plots also provide mini-cliff hangars within a story. If a protagonist is left in an uncertain position at the end of a chapter, you can break away, heightening the tension, something known as architectural suspense, which we'll come to next.

Ian Rankin, the genius behind the Detective Inspector Rebus books, is a master of the sub-plot. While Rebus is off solving some gruesome murder, another plot is bubbling in the background. Rankin leaves you unsure as to how it will link with the main plot until the very end. The Hanging Garden is an example of a book with excellent sub-plotting.

Extra reading

Sanderson recommends a short essay by screenwriter Terry Rossio, entitled "Strange Attractor", and having read it myself, recommend it highly. In short, Rossio believes that a story needs to have a good concept, something compelling, enticing, attractive. It's not easy to think of something original nowadays—if only we were doing this a hundred years ago, eh? But try we must. You might find it helpful.

III. Architectural Suspense

"The suspense is terrible. I hope it will last."
Willy Wonka, *Charlie and the Chocolate Factory*

We've all read that novel where at some point you put it down and forget it ever existed. It failed to grip you, to compel you to go on. Often the culprit is a lack of suspense—the glue that binds the reader's hands to the covers.

An effective tool exists for generating suspense. It goes by the name **'architectural suspense'**.

"The writer's duty is to set up something that cries for a resolution and then to act irresponsibly, to dance away from the reader's problem, dealing with other things, prolonging and exacerbating the reader's desperate need for a resolution." Sol Stein, *Stein* On Writing

It's funny how in reality we try our best to avoid anxieties and conflict. In fiction, we seek them out. There's a degree of excitement involved in watching someone deal with a tricky situation. It grips us. We want to see if they can get out of it. We live through them. There are other reasons too. Perhaps it makes us feel better about ourselves, that if someone relatable is going through a stressful time it almost feels as if we're not alone, that we can do the same.

To create stressful situations for our characters in which readers skim lines with wide eyes, tearing pages in their haste to turn them, is a wonderful skill. We've hooked our reader, enchanted them. We don't want that spell to end, and neither do they. One way to keep it going is with architectural suspense.

So what is architectural suspense? In short, it's using plot and story structure to create suspense, creating different suspenseful threads to leave the reader on tenterhooks. Let's illustrate it with a few examples.

Chapter one of James Barclay's novel, *Noonshade*, ends with a siege at breaking point. We're left with the thoughts of a character named Barras, who suggests he has a few tricks up his sleeve to turn the tide. Of course, Barclay is too smart to reveal what they are there and then. Instead, he draws it out.

The following chapter shifts the story to a different set of characters hundreds of miles away. Annoying at first, but it made me want to read on, to get through the chapter to see what happens at the end of the first. Chapter two ends with another cliff hanger. Then comes chapter three and back to Barras, all the while I want to know what happens to those in chapter two. And so the **cycle of suspense is born.**

Another master of this method is George R.R. Martin. I call him a master not just for the quality of his use of plotting, character, and structure, but for the scale of the story he's weaving. A beautiful tapestry. If you're not familiar with his story structure, each chapter follows the perspective of a different character, and there are loads of them. Some characters feature more than others—Daenerys, Jon, Tyrion, Arya, Jaime, to name a few. Without wishing to stir controversy, these are the more significant and intriguing characters. Countless times I found myself motoring through the chapters of other 'lesser' characters just to get to the next one about Tyrion.

Wouldn't some kind of template for this method be useful? Indeed it would, and editor of some of the greatest contemporary books, Sol Stein, has provided it:

Chapter 1: The chapter ends with a turn of events that leaves the reader in suspense. The reader wants to stay with the characters and action of that chapter.

Chapter 2: The reader finds themselves in another place and/or with a different character. The reader still wants to know what happens in Chapter 1. Chapter 2 ends with a turn of events that leaves the reader in suspense. The reader wants to know how Chapter 2 turns out.

Chapter 3: Picks up after Chapter 1. The reader is still in suspense following Chapter 2. By the end of Chapter 3, a new line of suspense has been created.

To follow this over successive chapters will leave the reader in a continuous state of suspense. There will likely be no sag in the middle of the story, though it runs the risk of fatiguing the reader. It really all depends on the type of story you want to tell.

So in short, what we can take from this technique is that **chapter endings should arouse the reader's curiosity to discover what happens next.**

As writers, I think we kind of instinctively know to do this. But what else can we do to heighten the suspense? Stein recommends carrying out the brutal task of cutting the weakest scene. From his editor's perspective, he's of the view that doing so will strengthen the story.

He also recommends cutting out or minimising the narrative summaries which happen between scenes — the boring stuff we don't really care *that* much about, like travelling hundreds of miles, crossing through meadows of golden wheat and fields of swaying emerald grass, through whispering woods and over rolling hills (see what I mean?).

IV. The Crucible

The crucible is a simple and effective plotting tool. At its core is the relationship between the protagonist and the antagonist. The conflict between them spawns plot. It illustrates wonderfully the interwoven relationship enjoyed between character and plot.

What is a crucible?

A crucible is an environment—emotional, physical, mental—that bonds two people together, namely the protagonist and the antagonist. It often takes the form of a relationship or location.

Moses Malevinsky in *The Science of Playwriting* (1925), said the crucible is 'the pot, or the furnace, in which the drama is boiled, baked, stewed, or hibernated'. It is, he says, 'one of the most important elements of [a story's] organic structure'.

James N. Frey defines it as 'the container that holds the characters together as things heat up; the bond that keeps them in conflict with one another.'

Without a crucible to contain the characters there can be no conflict, and without conflict, there is no drama. The master playwright Lajos Egri said that opposing characters bonded together 'won't make a truce in the middle and call it quits'. They are committed to the continuing conflict until there is a final resolution: the Dark Lord defeated, the Ring destroyed, the demon gateway closed. Sol Stein said:

> 'The key to the crucible is that the motivation of the characters to continue opposing each other is greater than their motivation to run away. Or they can't run away because they are trapped, for instance in a prison cell, lifeboat, island, or by family.'

If anything, as the story develops and the conflicts deepen, the characters should be locked further into the crucible.

Conflicting bonds

You know your characters are *not* locked in a crucible when the reader is liable to ask, "Why doesn't the knight just go home and forget about the dragon?" To avoid this, the character must be bonded to their task, quest, or job.

In the epic medieval poem *Ser Gawain and The Green Knight*, Gawain, an honourable knight of King Arthur's roundtable, agrees to the challenge of the Green Knight to behead him. The condition is that a year on from that day, Gawain is to find the Green Knight and allow him to do the same. Gawain agrees, beheads the Green Knight, who picks up his head and leaves.

A rather shocked Gawain cannot just walk away from his task. He has given his word, and to a knight of the roundtable, his word is everything. Who would dare risk being called dishonourable in such circumstances? Death would be a better choice. So Gawain sets out to find the Green Knight, and not once do we doubt the legitimacy of his cause. Gawain and the Green Knight are locked in a crucible.

Let's take the example of a character whose job is making her ill. "Why doesn't she just quit?" we ask.

What if she's a single mother with three kids to support? Kids who have worn the same school uniforms for so long their trousers look like shorts. Each day they come home with cheeks wet with tears and tales of mockery that break her heart. Our character is locked in a crucible with her job.

Keep the question in mind: **where's the crucible?** It helps to consider character motives when doing so. The character must be well-motivated to see their goal through to the end. Some examples from the literary world:

The Old Man and the Sea by Hemingway. The old man cannot let go of the fish, and the fish cannot shake him. They are bonded together, but not just by hook and line, but by the old man's need to prove his manhood and his skills as a fisherman. Only death will free them from the crucible.

The Lord of the Rings by Tolkien. Frodo can't just toss the One Ring into the Anduin River and head back to the Shire. Sauron would find it, return to power and wreak destruction on Middle Earth, Shire and all. Frodo carries that moral burden, but also the corruption of the ring. He is bound in a crucible with the ring by his need to destroy it.

The Eye of the World by Jordan. Rand cannot just turn around and head back to Emond's Field. Ba'alzamon haunts his dreams, stalks his shadow. He is locked in a crucible with the Dark One by his need to uncover the truth of who he is and what fate has in store.

Some other examples of crucibles:

- A father and son in conflict with each other. Neither can walk away; they are bonded by familial love. Love is their crucible.
- Cell-mates in a prison can easily run into conflict with each other, conflict difficult to escape from. The prison cell bonds them together and forms their crucible.
- The situation is similar for people stranded on a boat or on an island. The boat or island is their crucible.

A possible formula

I always try to think of handy ways to remember things, and in this instance, I think a formula may help.

Protagonist+Antagonist+Conflicting Bonds=Crucible

Another example:

Son+Father+Familial Love=Crucible

Ways of creating a crucible

- Can you change the **location** of the scene to one in which it's more difficult for the participants to leave? Two enemies trapped in an elevator. Young boys forced to play with each other while their widowed parents spend some time alone.
- Think about the **backstories of your characters**. What links could you include to lock them in a crucible? Love and relationships are big ones for many people. Jobs too. Or a

sense of duty or justice, such as serving in the police force or military, or being Batman.

You may find this technique doesn't work for you, and that's fine. Lessons can be gleaned from everything, even small ones, and what we can take from this, above all, is to think about the relationship between protagonist and antagonist and the need to continue the conflict and intensify the between them.

V. Twisting the Knife: Creating Tension

Can you think of a moment in a book when you lost all awareness of your surroundings? The only thing that mattered was happening there on the page. When at last the tension relents, you come up for air and utter a "fuck."

As with conflict, we seek to create lives free of tension, yet in fiction the opposite is true. Indeed, it can be scientifically proven. When we read pages such as those laden with tension, a hormone is released into our bloodstream, similar to adrenaline, which stimulates the heart and increases blood pressure, in turn provoking an excitable feeling, a feeling readers grow to crave.

But like most things, too much ruins it, and you can run the risk of boring the reader. That's why, at this early point in the chapter, it's important to set out the difference between suspense and tension. Suspense, as we know from the previous chapters, can span across large parts of the story, even an entire book. Tension can last a few lines, a paragraph, perhaps a sequence of scenes.

Think of tension as an elastic band. The more it's stretched the looser and weaker it becomes until eventually, it snaps. Use too much tension and you'll break the elastic band in your reader's head.

How do you create tension?

One way to create tension is to include **strange, mysterious, or chilling facts**. Check out this sentence from The Day of the Jackal by Fredrick Forsyth.

> "It is cold at 6:40 in the morning of a March day in Paris, and seems even colder when a man is about to be executed by firing squad."

How did you feel reading this sentence? Did you want to know more? Did questions pop into your mind? Who is being executed? And for what? Why that time of day? All of these questions create tension and encourages us to keep reading.

Friction is another way to build tension. Think of situations or people that don't go together, a clash of opposing forces. An example would be a Hasidic Jew sharing a prison cell with a neo-Nazi. Another may involve two office workers who hate each other's guts being stuck in an elevator.

Dialogue is another effective method of creating tension. Confrontational dialogue can have readers turning pages faster than someone reading a magazine in an oncologist's waiting room. Think about all those times you've seen an argument in the street. "I wonder what they're arguing about?" people always mutter as they crane their necks to get a better look. People enjoy watching conflict.

Using tension early on in a book or story can allow the writer to gain more control of the reader's emotions. In provoking excitement, the reader may become a more willing passenger on your journey.

One thing you can do to spark some tension is to **move a specific sentence to another location**. The purpose is to stretch out the tension as much as possible. Here's an example from Stein:

> "I was heading over to Uncle Urek's before I got your message. He in trouble again?"
> A fog of silence descended. Nobody looked at anybody else. Finally, Feeney said, "She doesn't know."

How about moving one line?

> "I was heading over to Uncle Urek's before I got your message."
> A fog of silence descended. Nobody looked at anybody else.
> "He in trouble again?"
> Finally, Feeney said, "She doesn't know."

Notice the difference? Simple and effective.

Twist the knife

To create tension is a brilliant thing, like sparking a fire. But it's easy to let the flames gutter out. As mentioned above, too much tension can fatigue a reader. Finding the right balance, I think, comes with experience. One way to get that experience is to play about with dangling the carrot in front of the reader's nose, showing them the resolution and then taking it away.

Think of an incident, real or fictional, where a pressing situation arises, but all of a sudden it's over, the tension gone.

You hear the keys of a piano jingle in the next room, but you're alone in the house. Your heart freezes, but you toughen your resolve and pull open the door. The cat runs out.

How could the tension be prolonged? Could the character get a phone call, one they must answer before they can investigate further, or does someone knock on the front door as they're about to enter the room?

Plotlines that create tension

Sol Stein put together a handy list of examples, and here they are:

- **Dangerous work is involved.** A soldier on the front line; a space engineer repairing the outside of a ship. When writing this kind of story or scene, exploring the tiny details of the type of work involved increases and prolongs tension.
- **A deadline is nearing.** 'You've got twenty-four hours, or the girl gets it.' Deadlines are used in many clever ways. James Barclay used one in Noonshade, where a portal to the realm of dragons is inching open, meaning the heroes must race to close it before hordes of fire-breathing man-eaters invade Balaia.
- **An unfortunate meeting occurs.** Someone from a character's past reappears, perhaps an old enemy or lover. Or running into the wrong person at the wrong time.

- **An opponent trapped in a closed environment**. Stein gives a wonderful example here, which I'll paraphrase: A lion has escaped its enclosure in the zoo and chases a woman into a cellar storeroom. The ageing zoo ranger is the only one onsite with a rifle. When he arrives at the scene a younger man offers to take the rifle and the old man gives him it, not one to kill animals. As the pair are about to descend into the cellar the younger man begins to shake. His loose grip of the weapon reeks of inexperience. The ranger offers to take it back, and the younger man hands it over. At the head of the cellar stairs, the ranger hears the lion below, but can't see anything in the gloom. Holding the rifle with one hand he takes out a torch. He struggles to balance both the rifle and torch, tries to hold the latter in his mouth, but it's too big. As he puts the torch down the lion bounds up the cellar steps.

In this last example, Stein keeps on increasing and stretching out the tension. First, the old man hands over the rifle. The younger man then hands it back. Then the old ranger struggles to see into the cellar, struggles using both rifle and torch, until at last the lion leaps. Wouldn't it be so much more boring if he arrived, looked into the cellar and the lion jumped at him?

So a few summary points on tension:

- Ask how can you elasticate the tension? Stretch it too much, though, and it may break your story.

- Consider adding steps or detours within scenes to prolong tension. Anything that keeps the end at bay.

- Using tension early on in a story can grab hold of the reader's emotions.

- Chilling language, dialogue, sentence structure, and conflicting or confrontational situations can all create tension.

VI. Character Plotting

I hummed and hawed over where to put this chapter. Why here, at the end of the section on plotting? To remind you that character makes plot. When we plot we think of ways to test our characters, and this is the final stage. This is the trial run, them walking through it. Their emotional journey. The highs and the lows. Your characters will undoubtedly change the course of the plot as you test them, as you learn more about them. This process, in essence, is the final course of plotting. Ensuring the plot is consistent with the characters.

I'm a bit of a planner. I need a framework, something to help keep my eye on the endgame. When it comes to writing, I often begin a story or chapter by mapping it out in as much detail as I can think of. In the past, most of my planning focused on plot, moving the story from A to B. While I include character development in this, it never had a focal role.

The more I write, the more my appreciation for the significance of characterisation grows. Nowadays, as part of that planning exercise, I carry out something I've coined a **character plot**.

Character plots?

Like plotting out a story using events, instead, I map out the story using my characters' emotional journey—their thoughts, feelings and desires—as those events unfold.

Emotion is so important in our lives, and in our characters' lives too. Playwright Moses Malevinsky summed it nicely in *The Science of Playwrighting:*

> "*Emotion, or the elements in or of an emotion, constitute the basic things in life. Emotion is life. Life is emotion. Therefore emotion is drama. Drama is emotion.*"

To echo that point, another fantastic playwright, Lajos Egri, said, "emotion, to be sure, is as necessary to a [story] as barking to a dog."

Why is this emotional journey regarded as so important? Let's look at the potential reaction to a simple email.

As writers, we send our work off to publishers in the hope of making some cashish, reaching new readers, enriching peoples' lives with our words. When we see the response email from a publisher in our inbox our hearts begin to flutter. Is it good news or bad? You open the email, skim the words, seeking the ones you want, the ones that will tell you everything you need to know. 'Congratulations' or the dreaded 'unfortunately'.

In that brief moment, we are filled with hope and in the fleeting seconds after we're either dejected or elated. Emotions swing violently to either end of the spectrum. All from one little email.

What's the benefit of character plotting?

Put yourself in your character's shoes. Think of all of the massive, life-changing events you drag them through. How would it feel to be them? The highs, the lows, the anxieties, the uncertainties, the pressure to perform and succeed. I do not doubt your characters will go through some intense shit in your stories. Plotting their emotional journeys may help you get to grips with each and every swing of emotion.

It can help make characters and the events that happen to them more believable. If a character kills someone for the first time, that's a pretty massive thing to do. Playing God. Snuffing out the light of life. To really get at the heart of what your character is thinking and feeling, taking the time to plot out that emotional journey is going to help you achieve that.

It also serves as a checks and balance in case any emotional reactions that you'd expect a character to go through do not get addressed, or aren't properly addressed. You're not chancing things. You're thinking them through in excellent detail. All of this is only going to benefit both your story and your characters.

How do you go about it?

I speak entirely from personal experience. What works for me may not work for you. The trick is trial and error: try something, see if it works, try something else... and so on, until you hit your winning formula.

I always begin by planning the story. In my mind, I need to know the events that are going to happen and the destination I'm headed to. Once I know the key events, I turn to my characters, embed myself in their minds and walk the path I've constructed for them. I jot down any little feelings that spring to mind as I progress through the plot.

These emotional reactions, in turn, shape the plot. The characters we create are full of surprises. As they come to life with their own thoughts and feelings, they manipulate the flow of the story as it unfolds, meaning you're not tying yourself up in knots when inconsistencies arise between plot and character. The two are very much linked and determine the fate of each other.

In summary, a character plot can be a useful exercise because:

- In plotting the emotional turmoil of your character, you're leaving no stone unturned, making for more believable, empathetic characters.
- Mapping out both the story and the character's emotional journey can help shape both, which will lead to a more engaging and less disjointed story.
- It gives more structure to your story. Knowing how to get from A to B is one thing, knowing how your character feels about it is another. Your overall plot and characterisation will be stronger as a whole.

Give it a go and see what you think.

Premise

I. The Importance of Premise

It's interesting how attitudes change. When I first began writing I viewed the plot as the cornerstone of a story. If characters live a static existence, then what's the point? The more time I invested in improving my writing, I realised the error of my ways. Character is, in fact, king. It's their conflicts, their struggles, their journeys that glue hands to books and eyes to pages.

But recently I came across something that made me question whether I was, in fact, wrong again. The element that arguably presides over them all is something I never paid much attention to, something I rather hoped emerged from my stories rather than weaved it into their fibre. The king of kings, the emperor, the god, is the **premise.**

What you'll read below is just a theory, like any other. One that's persuaded me. It's not a hard and fast rule. What you take from it is down to you.

Premise?

Yeah, premise. AKA theme, goal, purpose, central idea, thesis ... I could go on. None of these words really encapsulate the meaning quite like premise, though. Let's nab a definition form the Oxford English Dictionary:

Premise (noun)

1. A previous statement or proposition from which another is inferred or follows as a conclusion.

   '*if the premise is true, then the conclusion must be true*'

2. An assertion or proposition which forms the basis for a work or theory.

   '*the fundamental premise of the report*'

It's the second definition which I think suits the writer best: *an assertion or proposition which forms the basis for a work or theory.*

Now, not all stories have to explore a premise or theme. Some stories are just damn good tales. The books that have remained alive in my mind longest, though, have been the ones that have explored a premise, sought to explore a point and bring clarity to it, such that when you put the book down you feel like you've learned something. That's what I want my writing to do, the kind that can help people, and hopefully, make a difference.

The premise is the sat nav. It will show you the way, lead you to a satisfying conclusion. It will suggest the one and only road the story should follow. Alexandre Dumas summed it up nicely:

> *"How can you tell what road to take unless you know where you're going?"*

I'm still not really buying it...

I don't blame you.

But wait.

Most of the time, a story has a *point*, a *purpose*, a *goal*— words we established are intertwined with premise. If there's no goal, how can a story work sequentially toward a conclusion? How do you know what steps to take to build your way to the end?

The premise, in essence, is the path to the conclusion. It is the argument you want to put across, the conviction you want to make. The plot, the characters... they're all just vehicles for getting you there. Cannon fodder. You bend and manipulate them so you can state your purpose, make your point, prove your premise.

Still not having it? Some examples might help.

Romeo and Juliet

This is a play about love. But it's no ordinary kind of love. It's a love so great that it transcends death. Rom and Jules couldn't be together in the living realm, so chose to be with each other in that of the dead. The premise here is *great love defies even death.*

Othello

When O to the O discovers a handkerchief belonging to Desdemona in Cassio's home, envy consumes his heart. He kills Desdemona and then himself. The premise here is *jealousy destroys itself and the object of its love.*

This still isn't very clear...

Let's break down premise into its core components. In 1946, the Hungarian playwright Lajos Egri published *The Art of Dramatic Writing.* His first chapter is on premise. It changed everything for me. It all made so much sense. If you can get a hold of a copy of this book, do it.

> *"The very first thing you must have is premise. And it must be a premise worded so that anyone can understand it as the author intended it to be understood. An unclear premise is as bad as no premise at all."*

Egri was very much of the view that premise provided direction, a way to get to the conclusion of the story. Characters and plot are the vehicles to get there and the fuel required to propel them to that end is conflict. It is these three elements — **character, conflict, conclusion**—that Egri says every premise must have.

Let's clear this up with an example:

Great love defies even death.

The premise of Romeo and Juliet. Can you identify each element in this sentence?

Great love represents character. *Defies* suggests conflict. *Death* is the conclusion.

Make sense? Let's try another:

Frugality leads to waste.

Frugality represents character. *Leads to* suggests conflict. *Waste* suggests the conclusion.

Knowing a premise must have these three ingredients makes things *so* much easier, don't you think? And these short, snappy sentences make for a fine thumbnail synopsis for your story. Here are a few other examples. Can you identify each element?

Honesty defeats duplicity.
Dishonesty leads to exposure.
Ill-temper leads to isolation.
Egotism leads to loss of friends.
Bragging leads to humiliation.

Don't run off in joyous abandon just yet. There's something else Egri says a premise must have, and that's **conviction.**

A premise cannot be a question. It's a statement. It doesn't have to be a universal truth, but you, or at least your characters, must wholeheartedly believe it.

"Until [the author] takes sides, there is no [story]. Only when he champions one side of the issue does the premise spring to life."

So in effect, you could pick a premise such as *killing your dog leads to happiness,* and as long as you can establish and prove it in your story, that's a legitimate premise. Egri was of the view that if you did not wholeheartedly believe in your premise then you would be destined to fail. I don't share that view as long as you can immerse yourself in the mind of someone who does. It's certainly easier if it's something you do believe, though.

Can a story have more than one premise? Egri says no. It ultimately leads to confusion. *"Nobody can build a [story] on two premises, or a house on two foundations."* I'm a never say never kind of guy, though, so if you can make it work, go for it.

Right or wrong?

You may disagree with every word I've scribbled here. I entirely understand if that's the case. The most wonderful thing about writing is there is no right or wrong way to do it. Some people never write with a premise in mind, others reveal it during editing, and some cannot start without. What works for someone may not work for you. All I say is, give it a go. Write a short story beginning with a premise. Build your characters and plot around it and let the premise direct you. Then make up your mind.

II. Finding a Premise

As we've seen in the last chapter, a premise-led story takes a hard look at the meaning of things, examines a deep-rooted idea. In novelist John Gardner's view, it's only when the writer considers the premise of a story "does he achieve not just an alternative reality, or loosely, an imitation of nature, but true, firm art—fiction as serious thought."

We've had a look at the essence of premise, now it's time to consider further some ways or picking a premise, weaving them into your tales and lastly, uncovering those that may already lay hidden within your writing.

Coming up with a theme

Almost the opposite to what we saw Lajos Egri argue in the previous chapter, John Gardner (who had the interesting middle name 'Champlin') argued that premise is not imposed on a story, but rather evoked from within it. Initially it's intuitive, but finally becomes an intellectual consideration on the part of the writer.

It seems there's no straight answer. When you seek out examples of premises you'll invariably find lists of single-word suggestions. It's important to remember that while it's helpful to summarise a premise in this way, it's quite a reductionist approach. I've found it more helpful to think of it as a type of essay question you'd find in school or university. You're asked to explore or criticise a concept, and in essence, you're doing the same with your theme.

It should be borne in mind that a premise should not be a question; it's the answer. How the answer is arrived at is the story. Here are a few examples of some premise topics and ideas for more specific premises:

- **Alienation** – the effects of it; how to fight it.
- **Betrayal** – how it feels; attitude changes to friends and loved ones.
- **Coming of Age** – the loss of childhood innocence; the shift from childhood to adulthood, or; a significant step in personal growth.
- **Courage** – the courage to face adversity, to deal with conflict; the development of or the loss of it.
- **Discovery** – discovering new places; uncovering information, inner meaning, inner strength, treasures.
- **Death** – how to escape it; facing it; dealing with the effects of it.
- **Fear** – conquering it; coping with it; the crippling effects of it.
- **Freedom** – losing it; longing for it; striving to achieve it; fighting for it.
- **Good Versus Evil** – the struggle between the two opposing forces; the triumph of one over the other.
- **Justice** – the fight for it; injustices; seeking the truth.
- **Loss** – of life, innocence, possessions, freedoms.

- **Love conquers all** – love provides the motivation to overcome an obstacle.
- **Religion** – the effect religion has on individuals; how beliefs shape their lives; faith; extremists such as cults, sin, the afterlife.
- **Power** – gaining it; handling it; losing it; fighting for it.

Questions to ask

If you feel like your premise isn't getting the focus you want it to, there are two helpful questions you can ask yourself. These can be pondered at any stage of the writing process— planning, drafting or editing.

1. What is the meaning of things?
2. What deep-rooted idea is being examined?

Examining your manuscript with these in mind can help to maintain all-important structure and direction.

Revealing premise

Revealing a premise is a subtle art. A concern for writers is the possibility of readers not picking up on the clues, so in a panic, make it too obvious. Let's look at some examples.

The theme of nakedness provides quite an illustrative example. One detail that could be used to suggest this theme is to feature chipping paint on a wall, or perhaps a character who wears very little clothing, or who is very open with their emotions. You could use contradictions which help to contrast the theme, known as a counter. So for instance, having a character who wears too much clothing, regardless of the weather.

In one of my own stories in which I sought to explore the conflict between choosing paths of good and evil, I had a spinning weather vane, unable to settle on any direction.

I have no doubt you can get creative with how you reveal your premise. Experiment and have fun.

Dialogue

One of the writer's most effective tools is dialogue. A story with little or no dialogue can sometimes make the eyelids flicker. Too much dialogue may leave the reader breathless. There seems to be one pervading guideline when it comes to writing dialogue, and that is **clarity is king.** Let's have a look why.

Presentation

Writers have different stylistic preferences when it comes to dialogue. The best approach I've found, and by best I mean the approach readers find clearest, is to use speech marks (") as opposed to a single apostrophe ('). Why? If, for instance, a character is speaking and quotes someone else, a single quotation mark can be used within the speech marks, therefore avoiding any confusion, for example:

> "I can't believe she called me 'an ungrateful cow.' She's got some nerve."

Another helpful approach to maintain clarity is to begin dialogue on a new line **whenever a new character speaks.** For instance:

> "Who was at the door?" Nick asked.

"A couple of Mormons," Sarah said.

Similarly, if a character reacts to something another character says or does, to maintain clarity, pop the reaction on a new line, followed by dialogue. So for example:

"We're all sold out," Dan said.
Jim sighed. "Have you not got any in the back?"

Attribution

An attribution, also known as an identifier, is the part of the sentence that follows a piece of dialogue. For example: 'John said.' In his creative writing lectures, Brandon Sanderson shares a few useful tips.

- Try to place the attribution as early as possible to help make it clear in the reader's mind who is speaking. This can be done mid-sentence, such as: "I don't fancy that," Milo said. "What else do you have?" Breaking like this works well if a character is going to be speaking for a few lines or paragraphs. You can also use an attribution before the dialogue, though there's something about this which I find jarring. Used sparingly it works well, but too often just seems annoying and archaic. It's all personal preference though.
- Try using beats, but not too many. What's a beat? A beat is a reaction to something said or done. So, for example, facial expressions like frowning, smiling, narrowing of the eyes, biting of the lip, hand gestures such as pointing, clenching fists, fidgeting. And then you've got physical movements, like pacing up and down, smashing a mug, punching a wall.

- Don't worry about over-using 'said' and 'asked'. To the reader, these words are almost invisible. What they care about is who exactly is speaking.

- When a character first speaks refer to them by name, but after that, it's fine to refer to them as he or she, provided they're still the one speaking. It's even desirable to use the pronoun; repeating a name over and over can irritate a reader.

Something I've noticed some of my favourite writers do, James Barclay and George R.R. Martin in particular, is, when possible, avoid using an attribution altogether. Less is more, as they say. If just a couple of people are talking, it may already be clear from the voices and language of the characters who exactly is speaking.

Again, to aid clarity, if there are more than two people involved in a conversation, it helps to use an attribution whenever a different character speaks. Nobody wants to waste time re-reading passages to check who's speaking. I don't enjoy it and I'm sure others don't either.

A repetitive use of attribution may grate on a reader. It can suggest a lack of trust in them to follow the story. It helps when editing to look for moments where you can take an attribution away, as well as looking for unclear sections where it might be necessary to add one.

A brief point on the styles of attribution. If you read a lot, you may notice some writers prefer the order "John said," and some prefer "said John". Sanderson is of the view that the character's name should come first because that's the most important bit of information to the reader. But the likes of Tolkien adopted the latter version. It's all personal preference. Why not mix and match?

Fictional dialogue

A useful distinction to make is between everyday dialogue and the dialogue we find in fiction.

The chatter we hear in real life is full of rambling, repetitive sentences, grumbles, grunts, 'erms' and 'ahs', with answers to questions filled with echoes (repeating a part of the question posed, e.g. "How are you?" asked A. "How am I?" B answered).

When we think of the dialogue we read in books, it contains little of the things we find in these everyday exchanges. According to Sol Stein, there's a reason for this—it's **boring** to read.

If it holds no relevance to the story, we don't care if a character's cat prefers to eat at your neighbour's house instead of your own, or if they think their nail job isn't worth the money they paid, or if they think the window cleaner isn't cleaning their windows. There are some snippets we overhear on the street that are interesting—an unusual name, a section of a story we want to know more of. Rare diamonds in a mine miles deep. I've fallen into the trap of trying to achieve realistic dialogue and it makes for drawn-out scenes and boring exchanges.

According to Stein, **dialogue ought not to be a recording of actual speech, but rather a semblance of it.**

What is this semblance of dialogue why should we try and achieve it?

The ingredients of effective dialogue

When we scrutinise a person as they're talking (all the boring stuff aside) we discover a lot about their character: who they are, what they believe in, and sometimes, if they reveal them, their motives. We glean all this from word choice, sentence structure, choice of topic, their behaviour as they say something.

It's these little details we as writers must dig for, so when it comes to writing our own dialogue, we can use them to help with our own characters and, if possible, develop the plot. **The key to mastering dialogue, according to Stein, is to factor in both characterisation and plot.**

How do we do it? Let's look at some examples

Milford:	How are you?
Belle:	How am I? I'm fine. How are you?
Milford:	Well, thanks. And the family?
Belle:	Great

I had to stop myself from stabbing my eyes out with my pen. This example is mundane, riddled with echoes, and gives us no imagery about the characters involved. Plus, it gives no advancement of plot. How about this version?

Milford:	How are you?
Belle:	Oh, I'm sorry, didn't see you there.

Milford:	Is this a bad time?
Belle:	No, no. Absolutely not.

See the difference? Milford asks Belle a question, which Belle doesn't answer. This is an example of **oblique dialogue**. It's indirect, evasive, and creates conflict, thereby moving the plot along. Oblique language helps to reveal a bit about the characters and the plot, namely that Belle could be a bit shifty and up to something unsavoury.

As a little exercise, try and think of some oblique responses to the following line. I'll give you an example to start. Remember to factor in Stein's key ingredients—**characterisation and plot**:

Exercise: "You're the most beautiful woman I've ever seen."

Example: "Did you say the same thing to that blonde girl behind the bar?"

In this example, we get a response which avoids answering the statement. She could quite easily turn around and say "Thank you," but that's boring. Instead, we're wondering about this man and what he's about, and a bit more about the woman too, namely that she's observant.

For another example of oblique dialogue, we can look to the one of the new Star Wars films, *The Last Jedi*. If I'm brutally honest, I thought much of the dialogue in this film was poor. It was far too informative, revealing details known to each character but said for the convenience of moving the plot along.

However, there was one good instance of dialogue in there, which went something like this:

> Luke steps inside the Jedi temple where Rey is looking at a number of books upon a stone dais.
>
> "Who *are* you?" Luke asked.
>
> "What are these books?" Rey said.

It's this avoiding of the question that sparks a bit of tension. Is Rey hiding something? We don't know much about her and now we want to know more. The plot is advanced too because our attention is now on these books which may have some bearing on the rest of the story.

Voice

A character's voice is an important factor in dialogue. Nobody speaks in the same way. Some people have lisps, some people say their 'r's' like 'w's', some people don't enunciate properly, say words differently, speak in accents, have a nasal twang. There are *so* many variables. Introducing these features to some or all of your characters can help to make them more memorable and distinct.

Language

Linked to voice is the use of language. A person from a particular region might say words unique to them or that area. People from Liverpool, or Scousers as we're known, often refer to their friends as "lad", for example, "'ello, lad. How's it going?" Or we also often use "sound" instead of "good," for example: "How are you?" "I'm sound, thanks." It can add more layers to your story. But a few words of caution. Don't overcook it. Clarity is always king. Make sure it's easy to follow.

The same goes for the use of accents, like "Am goin' for a smoke. Ye comin'?" The last thing you want is to leave your reader frowning. Instead, you could describe the way they speak rather than express it. Sol Stein also warns against spelling out pronunciations, and after reading H.P. Lovecraft, I'm jumping up and down seconding that motion. Here's an extract from *Shadow over Innsmouth:*

> "Told about an island east of Otheite war they was a lot o' stone ruins older'n anybody knew anything abaout, kind o' like them on Panape... Nobody cud git aout o' them war they all got the stuff, an' all the other natives wondered haow they managed to find fish in plenty even when the very next islands had lean pickin's."

This type of dialogue goes on for about six or seven pages. I don't quite know how I got through it.

Pacing

Dialogue has a knack for increasing the pace of the story. Readers can find themselves tearing through pages laden with dialogue. As with all tools of the craft, it pays to know how best to use it. Literary agent Noah Lukeman said a writer must learn how to use restraint when it comes to dialogue, "to sustain suspense and let a scene unfold slowly."

Again, it's all a matter of preference.

Passive voice is okay

You've probably heard that you ought to avoid the passive voice as if it were the hand of a leprous beggar. We'll explore the passive voice in detail in the chapters to come. For now, know this: when it comes to dialogue, passive voice has a place.

In reality, most people when they speak use passive language. If a character speaks in a passive voice, it can be more real, genuine. Take this example:

> "I was going to come over to your house but I wasn't sure if you were in."

In this example there are three words that may be construed as passive, yet it works.

Informative dialogue

In his book *The First Five Pages*, Noah Lukeman says that one of his biggest reasons for rejecting a manuscript is the use of informative dialogue. In other words, using dialogue as a means for conveying information, or **info dumping**. He says it suggests the writer is lazy, too unimaginative to convey the information in a subtler way.

Sometimes dialogue will give us no information at all. Sometimes snippets. Often if you overhear a conversation between two people you'll find you understand little of what they discuss. It's the little details they reveal that are most interesting. Take the example of someone mentioning they went to the hospital. The person they're with may know why they went, but you don't. Give the reader pieces of the giant puzzle and leave them wanting more.

Lukeman suggests a few solutions to mend instances of informative dialogue. One is to highlight pieces of dialogue which merely convey information and do not reveal or suggest the character's personality or wants. Break them apart and find a way to let them trickle into the story.

Editing dialogue

For sound editing advice a good person to turn to is a master. In his book on the craft of writing, Sol Stein provides a very helpful checklist when going over passages of conversation:

- What is the purpose of this exchange? Does it begin or heighten an existing conflict, for example?
- Does it stimulate curiosity in the reader?
- Does it create tension?
- What is the outcome of the exchange? Does it build to a climax, or a turn of events in the story, or a change in relationship with the speakers?

One additional step Stein recommends is reading dialogue aloud in a monotone expression. Listen to the meaning of the words in your exchanges.

"What counts is not what is said but the effect of what it means... The reader takes from fiction the meaning of words. And above all, they take the emotion that meaning generates."

There's another question you can ask yourself: are the lines of each character consistent with their background? Everybody speaks in a different way: accents, phrases, sentence order. One way to show this variation is with the use of speech markers — signals in dialogue which the reader can quickly identify. For example:

- A well-educated person may use long, jargonistic words.
- Throwaway words and phrases. These could be used as a verbal tic.
- Tight or loose wording. An example would be "Beat it." The shortness suggests character traits to the reader.
- Run-on sentences. Useful when characterising a chatterbox or somebody not quite sane.
- Sarcasm.
- Omitted words. Used in novels to portray lower classes. "What you doing?"

So these are a few things that I've found helpful when it comes to writing dialogue. Perhaps the most important piece of advice I've taken away from them all is to always maintain clarity while using obliqueness to give dialogue that snappy, enticing edge. It's easier said than done, mind.

Viewpoint, Tense and Narrative Distance

In a shiny little nutshell, the viewpoint is the perspective through which the story is told. A lot of guides on viewpoint say there are three types of viewpoint. I'm going to say there are four: **first person, second person, third person limited, and third person omniscient.**

What perspective you choose is ultimately down to you and what suits your story best. So for instance, a story with a large cast of characters may better be told from the third person omniscient perspective, whereas a story about a hero may best be told from their perspective.

Let's take a look at each, before turning to tense and lastly, narrative distance.

First person

This is the viewpoint of 'I'.

"I picked up the sword and I chopped off his toes."

The first person has a present narrator, guiding us through the tale—what they see, think, feel. It's perhaps the most intimate of all viewpoints, the reader sharing the mind of your point of view (POV) character.

H.P. Lovecraft was a big fan of the first person form, and in my view, was a master of it. The manner in which he tells his tales makes the narrator feel almost invisible. Rarely does he use the word 'I'. On page one of chapter one of *The Call of Cthulhu* for example, 'I' is used just three times.

As with all viewpoints, there are benefits and downsides. Here are a few of the benefits:

- The intimate nature of this approach makes it easier to build empathy between reader and character. This can be particularly helpful if a character is something of an anti-hero.
- It's immediately immersive for the reader, the story grabbing them by the collar and pulling them into the action.
- If your story focuses on characters, it's a great way to shine that stage light right on them.

A few of the downsides:

- The narration of the tale is limited to that character. So for example, it may be disruptive for the reader to be told the thoughts or feelings of one character when the tale has been told through the eyes of another. A POV character ought to instead infer thoughts and feelings from the body language and facial expressions of others. Unless the story is about mind reading, in which case disregard this entire paragraph.

- When writing with 'I' it can be easy to slip into your own personal voice as opposed to the characters'. Stay vigilant!
- It can be tempting to over-indulge in thought or emotional reflection at the expense of moving the story forward.
- If the POV character isn't particularly likeable, engaging or charismatic the reader may lose interest.

Second person

The rarest of all tenses. The second person is the form you're reading now—the 'you's'. The narrator addresses the reader directly.

It's a popular form in blogs and non-fiction because it makes for a more engaging read. I hope.

Everything I've read on the second person in fiction hasn't been too complimentary. Literary agent Noah Lukeman in *The First Five Pages* states that "it's extremely stylistic and nearly impossible to keep up for more than a page or two." Sol Stein, master editor, in his book *On Writing* recommends just shelving this approach altogether when it comes to fiction.

Again, it's up to you and how you feel the story would best be served.

Third person limited

Also referred to as third person subjective, this viewpoint tends to be the default for many writers. Third person limited is similar to the first person in that the story follows the perspective of individual characters. However, instead of using 'I', prose is written in the form of 'he', 'she', and 'they', with the tense mainly past, though present sometimes too. Here are a couple of examples:

> "James ceased his commentary as something caught his eye. He turned abruptly, reached out, and yanked a small boy away from Borric's horse. James lifted the boy off the ground and looked him hard in the eyes." *Prince of Blood*, Raymond Feist.

> "Jon blew out the taper he carried, preferring not to risk an open flame amidst so much old dry paper. Instead he followed the light, wending his way down the narrows aisles beneath barrel-vaulted ceilings." *A Clash of Kings*, George R.R. Martin.

1984 by George Orwell, a very relevant book at the moment and way, way ahead of its time, is an example of a story written in third person limited. George R.R. Martin uses it in all books of *A Song of Ice and Fire*, so too does Raymond Feist in *The Riftwar Cycle* novels, James Barclay in *The Chronicles of the Raven* series ... we could list until nuclear warfare ends the world, which may not be far off, but we've all got better things to do. You get it. It's popular.

Here are a few **advantages** to using this viewpoint:

- It allows a writer to adopt numerous and unique perspectives, allowing for a wider scope to world-build, develop conflict and build tension, as well as enabling the reader to contrast thoughts and feelings.

- Everyone loves a character that grows from a nobody into a hero, and this perspective is a great way to take the reader on that journey, showing them the trials and tribulations a character endures.

- It's the preferred approach by many contemporary writers and publishers.

And the **disadvantages**:

- As with the first person, the narration is limited to the POV character. The behaviours of others can be observed, but thoughts not known. Similarly, knowledge is restricted to the POV character. For example, if a huntress has spent her entire life in the woods, with no knowledge of civilization, the narration would seem a bit odd if she started to describe great cities and their histories.

Third person omniscient

As with third person limited, a story told this way is still about 'he', 'she' and 'they', but the narrator tells the reader the thoughts and emotions of all, or a large number, of characters. Omniscient follows an all-knowing narrator, whereas limited follows the tale of one or a few characters. If anything, limited lies closer to the first person.

It can be quite a demanding approach, but in the right hands works tremendously well. Tolkien was a fan. He tended to stick to the POV's of a handful of characters—Sam, Frodo, Aragorn (to name a few)—though dips into the minds of others too. I'd say he falls into the realm of the in between. A blend of both. Adrian Tchaikovsky is another writer who I'd say adopts the same approach. A mix of the two/ can be very useful.

The **advantages**:

- You can describe your world without restraint because you are god and you know all. It does not matter if your protagonist has never been somewhere, you can describe it down to the last detail.

The **disadvantages**:

- It can get quite demanding exploring the thoughts of all or a group of characters. Your story may go from a hundred thousand words to a series of encyclopaedic volumes.
- Stories told in this form are regarded as quite slow.
- According to Penguin Random House, it's fallen out of favour with some publishers, mainly because it's quite an old fashioned style. Tchaikovsky proves otherwise, mind.
- One of the biggest drawbacks is that this viewpoint tends to 'tell' the story, instead of 'show' it.
- The narration can have something of a cold and distant feel, with the risk of little emotional depth and weak ties to characters.

A few tips on viewpoint from editors

Changing tenses during a story is cautioned, but not ruled out. Lukeman recommends sticking with one viewpoint until reaching a line break. Switching from first to third person within the same passage can be confusing for a reader. He's very much against switching viewpoint at all, but says that "if you feel compelled to switch, at least do it in a place that will make it less disorientating for the reader." He asks too why do you feel compelled to switch. Most times it's down to the POV character lacking something and encourages you to spend more time working on that character.

Related to the above point, Sol Stein says, "The choice of point of view is yours, but once you've decided, be sure that you stick to it as if your reader's experience of the story depended on it. Because it does."

Which should you use? Stein recommends the one you feel most comfortable with. Try them all, and see for yourself. "... if your work isn't satisfying you, you can always put the draft aside and re-write it from another point of view. If you've used third person, try first."

Tense

Tense and viewpoint are very much linked. Past and present are the most common forms of tense.

Past involves a narrator telling the story after it's finished. H.P. Lovecraft was a big fan of this — individuals who experienced or witnessed something disturbing, retelling their tale with perfect recall. Past is regarded as the easier of the two to write. It fits well with first person or third person limited and omniscient.

Present tense involves a narrator telling the story as it happens. This approach gives a sense of immediacy — things are happening now. It's not as common as past tense, mostly because it's seen as quite difficult to maintain at length. Short forms of fiction suit it very well, though plenty of novels have been written in such a way.

Narrative distance

At last, we arrive at our final destination, narrative distance. This term was coined by John Gardner in his book *The Art of Fiction*. In short, it refers to how close you choose to take the reader into the character's mind, or into the story. Think of it like the zoom of a camera. How much can be seen through the lense? You can move in and out, focusing on small things, or widening the scale to see the broader scene. Take this example:

> *"It was winter of 1858. A large man stepped into the blizzard."* The language here is quite vague; there's some distance between reader and character.

> *"Henry hated snowstorms."* This is a bit closer. Not only do we have a name, but we've learned something about this chap named Henry.

> *"God, how he hated these snowstorms."* This is closer still. Not only do we know he hates snowstorms, but we're also wondering why he hates them *so* much.

> *"Snow. Under his collar, inside his shoes, freezing his miserable soul."* Now we're staring Henry right in the face. We're in his head, feeling how he does.

How close you choose to make the story is ultimately up to you.

Prose

I. The Most Hated Writing Rules

In or around November 2018, the novelist Jonathan Franzen caused a bit of a stir. An old article he'd penned in which he espoused his '10 writing rules for novelists' resurfaced. Twitter, as it is want to do, exploded. It was obvious that these so-called rules had touched a nerve with many writers, and I wanted to find out why.

So I put the question to writers. I polled writing groups on Facebook and received a total of 199 responses. More individuals shared their thoughts in the comments on my original post.

While this research has its obvious limitations, the results are interesting all the same and help us take a critical look at prose and the many so-called rules that litter it.

The results

Answer	Number of votes
Never use passive voice	37
There's rules?	33

Excessive use of adjectives	25
No adverbs	18
Never start a sentence with...	17
Show don't tell	13
Begin sentences with conjunctions (and, but)	12
Follow these exact rules to the letter or you are a horrible writer and terrible person	11
Flashbacks are a no-no	8
Just let people write how they want	7
The rules are so that weak writers know how not to suck at writing	5
All nevers and alwayses	4
Don't info dump	3
Jonathan Franzen is an entitled prick and can get bent ;	2
Not using 'that' so much	2
Real writers don't follow any rules	1
Ending the sentence on a preposition	1
Total Votes	**199**

Passive voice

Sitting proudly at the peak is the rule against using the passive voice. Ah, the dreaded passive voice. A thorn embedded in my foot that I cannot seem to pull free. It's one of my more popular articles on my blog, which tells me it pisses other people off too.

Going off my dealings with the passive voice, it can be a tricky area of grammar to fully understand, and that's not the fault of writers. Much of the day to day language we use is passive. It's become a natural way to speak. Shaking that conditioning can be tricky. Will passive voice be looked at with less scorn in the years to come?

Let's see what writers had to say about it:

"Passive voice. I hate the generic "never use passive voice" advice, it's such bull. Passive voice has a place, it's just plain lazy to simply avoid it rather than learn it, it's a tool like any other." Anni Davison

"Passive voice is definitely the one I struggle with the most, I usually run my articles and books through Hemingway before submitting to try and cut some of it out. It just feels natural to write/talk that way." Samantha Davis

"I argued with my teachers as a little kid over passive voice. I don't subscribe to that "rule." Never did. Who is anyone to tell a writer how to write and craft their own sentence? It's insane and yes, sometimes it does sound better. Put down the red pen and just read and experience the story." Laura Jones

"The one that is most troublesome for me is the "don't ever use passive voice" rule, because it ultimately comes from a misunderstanding of what we use passive voice for in our language. The idea that "active voice" sentences are "active" and "passive voice" sentences are not is flawed. If I write "Jim threw the ball" or "the ball was thrown by Jim," both sentences are equally active. Both show a ball being thrown. The main difference between the two sentences is the subject, and that is the critical point to consider. When an editor starts red-lining passive voice sentences in a paragraph, what they often end up doing is replacing a single subject for many, in turn making the passage more convoluted and harder to follow." JM Williams

Passive voice has a chapter of its own, so we'll leave it there for now.

There's rules?

There are *some rules*, one of which is broken by this very suggestion. 'There *are* rules?'

This answer touches upon the reasons behind why I think people got so wound up by Franzen's list in the first place. If you look further down the list of answers, you'll notice a few similar ones: 'follow these exact rules to the letter or you are a horrible writer and terrible person', 'just let people write how they want', 'Jonathan Franzen is an entitled prick and can get bent ;)', 'real writers don't follow any rules.' To me, these all stem from annoyance.

Let's set the record straight, or as straight as it can be. Beyond the guiding principles of grammar and language, everything else is pretty much fluid. So-called 'rules' are forever being broken with brilliant effect. That's part of the beauty of writing. The creativity. The freedom to work without constraint, to take something old and make it new. So whenever you see someone use the word rule, translate it to mean guideline, technique, idea, advice. Not something set in stone.

What do other writers think?

"I hate rules. Advice is cool. Learn tools and when, how, and why to use them. Strive to be a great writer and write with intention. But don't let anybody tell you there is some set of rules that dictates good writing and separates it from that bad, 'cos that's just bullshit and it's going to steer you wrong." Kai Kiet Pieza

"I don't think it was Franzen's use of the word "rules" that annoyed people so much as the incredibly stupid advice he gave." DL Mackenzie. In response, Janette Collins says: *"Honestly I do have a problem with the use of the word rules. Creativity should not be governed by rules."*

"[Franzen] penned this for The Guardian almost a decade ago. In that time he's also published two novels, two collections of essays and a translation of Karl Kraus' memoirs. So whether you choose to pour scorn on them or not, they certainly work for him." Stevie Cherry.

"Know the rules so you know when and how to break them. Then break them with malice. That's the best writing advice I've received." Mary Caelsto-Lenker

"Thou MUST learn thy rules... that thou mayst know when they may be broken to the greatest effect." Aaron Gallagher

"I before E except after C has been disproved by science. Outside of that, read Strunk and White's The Elements of Style, Rules and guidelines are there to help us write. If they get in the way, let them slip. But if it feels or reads wrong, perhaps a look at the 'rules' will help." Frank Booker

"I liked all 10 rules. If you can't get over the word "rules" that's your own problem (not you specifically OP). They're obviously meant as guidelines, and they're good and useful guidelines to follow unless you know how and why you're breaking them." Bobby Lee

"The 10 rules are exactly what I have learned over the years. None of them are always true, and bending them is a lot of fun. Part of the art of writing is knowing about them and understanding why these guidelines exist, working with them when it helps the prose, and knowing when you don't have to listen." Katharine Southworth

To adjective or not to adjective?

This one's bandied about quite a lot—refrain from using adjectives. They do you no good. Supposedly.

I've looked into this rule quite a bit and what I've come to learn is that it refers more to *how* adjectives are used. Though I'm a believer in maximum freedoms in life, an unchecked use of adjectives does make for a tricky read. But again, that's not to say you can't do it. I challenge you to prove me wrong.

Again, adjectives will be looked at in more detail below.

Adverbs

Adverbs have a similar reputation to that of their cousin, the adjective. I've heard many a writer exclaim their annoyance at reading the advice on adverbs in Stephen King's *On Writing* only to then read one of his novels and find his story peppered with them.

The answer, I believe, is the same as with adjectives. It's *how* you use the adverb.

Never start a sentence with...

I don't see this thrown about too often, yet it's scored pretty high on the list. The suggestion 'begin sentences with conjunctions' ties into this too.

It's a 'rule' I'm aware of, but having read so many fantastic and award-winning writers who break it consistently I've come to see it as obsolete. Bollocks to it. Start a sentence any way you want.

Don't tell me. Show me

I expected this one to score a little higher on the list due to the number of complaints I see about it. Like some of the other 'rules' noted above, it seems to be how you use it. Telling certainly has its place, particularly in shorter stories, but showing the story as if through the eyes of the character has a wonderful impact. What do the writers think?

> *"People parrot "show don't tell" nowadays, not seeming to realize that there are parts that SHOULD be told. Otherwise, one's protagonists just grimace, tremble, shudder, flush and twitch their way through the entire story (which gets tiring as well as ludicrous). And sometimes there IS a third alternative to either 'telling' or 'showing' -- subtext!" Marya Miller*

> *""Show, don't tell!" (Yes, they do always seem to be shouting when they spout these so-called rules.) I've seen some rather extreme examples of this: "Don't tell us that his car is red; show us." *rolls eyes* How are we supposed to do that when all we have are the words?" Thomas Weaver*

I hope you've gained an insight into the chaotic beast that is prose. The chapters that follow look at some of these specific 'rules' discussed above, but first, we'll take a look at perhaps the best approach to writing prose I've come across.

II. The Orwellian Approach

Every writer has their own style of writing prose. As we've seen above, there's no right way to do it. It's by practising relentlessly and studiously that a writer uncovers their style. Everything you read in this section on prose are but mere guidelines. Take from it what you will. What you'll find in this chapter is a very good set of guidelines, courtesy of George Orwell.

Orwellian prose

Two styles of prose seem to dominate writing: clear, concise prose, referred to as 'Orwellian', or the 'clear pane of glass', and; florid, literary prose, referred to as the 'stained glass window'.

George Orwell in his essay, *Politics and the English Language*, set out what he thinks good prose ought to consist of, all the while attacking the political system for the destruction of good writing practices. He was very much against the over-complication of language, which at the time (1946), was the direction politics was taking, and unfortunately still takes today, but that's a whole other topic.

Orwell believed prose should be like looking through a clear pane of glass at the story unfolding on the other side. The writing should be invisible, drawing as little attention to itself as possible. The reader shouldn't have to stop to re-read a sentence due to poor construction or stumble over a word used in the wrong way.

Words should be chosen because of their meaning, and to make them clearer, images or idioms, such as metaphors and similes, should be conjured. He encouraged the use of 'newly invented metaphors' which *"assists thought by evoking a visual image"*.

Orwell encouraged writers to use the fewest and shortest words that will express the meaning sought. *"Let the meaning choose the word."* If something cannot be explained in short, simple terms, the writer does not sufficiently understand it.

It was a change in common language that provoked Orwell to write his essay. Pretentious diction—words such as phenomenon, element, objective, eliminate and liquidate—is used to dress up simple statements. He blamed politics for this, and how politicians adopt hollow words and phrases, mechanically repeating them over and over until they become meaningless. I'm sure we can all agree we're fed up of hearing such phrases. "Take back control" or "Make America great again."

Orwell provided six guidelines to consider when writing prose:

1. *Never use a metaphor, simile or other figure of speech which you are used to seeing in print;*
2. *Never use a long word where a short one will do;*
3. *If it is possible to cut out a word, always cut it out;*
4. *Never use the passive [voice] where you can use the active;*

5. *Never use a foreign phrase, a scientific word, or jargon word if you can think of an everyday English equivalent;*

6. *Break any of these rules sooner than say anything outright barbarous.*

I've always found these rules terrifically useful. They're simple to understand, sensible and produce effective results. Some of the wording does seem restrictive, though, particularly his use of 'never'. I think it's fair to say there is an emotive element behind Orwell's writing of these rules. He is angry and frustrated with the degradation in the language of society. It may explain his more stringent language. But the message shines through: Orwellian prose is that which is short, simple and crucially, understandable.

The stained glass window

So we have our clear pane of glass, what then is the stained glass window?

You can still see the story on the other side, but the stained glass is colouring it in interesting ways. Language and structure are florid and creative. It's used more in fancy literary fiction and requires a mastery of language to pull off. Brandon Sanderson refers to it as the artist's style of prose, whereas Orwellian prose he regards as the craftsman's style.

You've probably heard the phrase 'purple prose'. This is an attempt at creating a stained glass window, but the description and structure are poor.

A blend of the clear pane and stained pane can work well. Tolkien often adopted this, particularly with his descriptions, and other writers, Sanderson and David Gemmell to name but two, like to start chapters in a florid way before transitioning into the clear pane. I suppose it depends on the scene. In fight scenes, for example, simple language can serve better to avoid disrupting the reader's flow. When describing places, people or settings colourful language can really enhance what would otherwise be quite mundane passages.

III. Getting to Grips with Passive Voice

In this chapter we're going to return to our list of the most hated writing 'rules' and consider the one which took the crown: never use the passive voice. As we've seen in the previous chapter with Orwell's guidelines, he too recommended using the active voice. Below, we'll look at what the active voice is, what the passive voice is, and the instances in which the passive voice may indeed be suitable to use.

First, we must consider why there is such dislike toward the passive voice. Here are a couple of comments from participants in the research which summarise the feelings nicely:

> *"Passive voice is definitely the one I struggle with the most, I usually run my articles and books through Hemingway before submitting to try and cut some of it out. It just feels natural to write/talk that way."*

> *"I hate the generic "never use passive voice" advice, it's such bull. Passive voice has a place, it's just plain lazy to simply avoid it rather than learn it, it's a tool like any other."*

What can we take from these comments?

i) it's not a straightforward 'rule' to understand, and;

ii) this lack of understanding can lead to a fear of it.

The active/passive conundrum

A definition is always a handy place to start.

The active voice

An active sentence is one in which the *subject* of that sentence is performing an *action* (a verb). This action is usually received by an *object,* which comes after the action in the sentence's construction.

Let's look at an example:

Layla *(subject)* nocked *(verb/action)* the arrow *(object).*

Dave *(subject)* stood *(verb/action)* in dog shit *(object).*

In each sentence, the subject—a noun—is carrying out an action. Layla nocked, Dave stood. The verb follows immediately after the subject, and the object usually after the verb. **Essentially, the subject is carrying out an action within that sentence.** A way you can remember this, though it's not a universal rule, is S.V.O.—Subject-Verb-Object.

The passive voice

A sentence written in the passive voice is usually one in which the *action* is being done to the *subject.* The *subject* performs the *action* but the latter often comes after the former. As well as this, the *object* tends to come before the *action* (verb). A role reversal of sorts in comparison to the active voice. You could remember it like this, though again it's not a hard and fast rule: O.V.S—Object-Verb-Subject.

The subject of the sentence is therefore passive—it's not doing anything, save for sitting at the end of the sentence looking pretty. So for example:

> The king's rallying cry *(object)* was not responded to by *(verb/action)* anyone *(subject)*.

> The entire city *(object)* was flattened *(verb/action)* by the tsunami *(subject)*.

The active versions of each of these sentences would be:

> Nobody (*subject*) responded to (*verb*) the king's rallying cry (*object*).

> The tsunami (*subject*) flattened (*verb*) the entire city (*object*).

So what's wrong with the passive voice?

The passive voice gets a bad rap. From my experience, it seems 'active' prose is preferred by publishers and agents. The question has to be asked: why? I can see two key reasons.

1. Prose written in the active voice is more immediate and immersive, grabbing the reader and refusing to let go. As writers, we want to grab the reader's attention, and as readers, we want to be grabbed. Writing in this style is proactive and forcible. The subject of each sentence is carrying out an action.

2. Prose written in the passive voice can use up a lot more words. While this post is an examination of writing 'rules' and why we don't like them, I have to admit I am a fan of Orwell's guidelines, particularly number three: *if it is possible to cut out a word, always cut it out.* Let's take an example from before:

> *Passive:* There were a great number of dead leaves lying on the ground.

> *Active:* Dead leaves covered the ground.

Twelve words to just five.

In defence of the passive voice

You may have read advice telling you *never* to use the passive voice. Here's a better bit of advice: *never* listen to a rule that begins with the word 'never'.

> "*This rule does not, of course, mean that the writer should entirely disregard the passive voice, which is frequently convenient and sometimes necessary.*" William Strunk Jr.

It's a tool, like any other in the writer's arsenal, and it has its own purpose. You wouldn't use a hammer to cut a piece of timber in two.

Passive voice is at times necessary. **One such instance is when a particular word is required to be the subject of the sentence.** Let's take an example from Strunk:

> The dramatists of the Restoration are little esteemed today.

> Modern readers have little esteem for the dramatists of the Restoration.

If you're writing about the dramatists of the Restoration, then the top sentence would be suitable, meaning use of passive voice becomes necessary. If the sentence seeks to discuss modern readers, then the latter example works. So in short, the **subject of the sentence can dictate which voice to use.**

Ask yourself: does this sentence need to be active? For example, some people may construe this sentence as passive: "Gideon is a doctor." The subject, Gideon, isn't doing anything in this sentence so there's no need to use the active voice. It can be a question of **necessity. Does this sentence *require* the active voice?**

When using the passive voice, Strunk recommended avoiding constructing sentences in which one passive phrase relies on another. For example:

> *Gold was not allowed to be exported.*

In this instance, the passive phrases are 'was' and 'to be'. The problem with this type of sentence construction, according to Strunk, is the use of the subject (gold) to express the entire action, rendering the verb (exported) useless beyond completing the sentence. An alternative construction could be:

The export of gold was prohibited.

The passive voice and dialogue

My day to day language is full of passive words. It's reached the extent where I'm pretty much conditioned to use it when I speak. If you listen to others, the same applies. To achieve more natural sounding dialogue, the occasional passive word may help.

"I <u>was</u> going to come over, but I <u>wasn't</u> sure whether you <u>were</u> home."

If I'd typed this, I'd edit it. Saying it is another matter. I invest much less effort in speech, as those who've struggled to understand my mumbling will attest to.

Making passive prose active

If you feel like you use a lot of passive voice and want to use more active, there are a few things you can do.

A good starting point is to look out for the following words, though I must warn you that sentences containing these words *may* indicate passive voice; it is not conclusive. Other factors must be considered, for example, the subject of the sentence, as outlined above.

- Been
- Am
- Be
- Are
- Was
- To be
- Were
- Is
- Are
- Being

Re-structuring sentences

Keeping the basic formula for active sentences in mind, you could try restructuring your sentences, but remember this is just the typical structure. Some active sentences may break this rule.

Another thing to try is to find a better verb, one that says everything you need to in just one word. They're out there, somewhere, though sometimes it feels like the hunt for Atlantis. It's such a good example, here it is a third time:

Passive: There were a great number of dead leaves lying on the ground.

Active: Dead leaves covered the ground.

Introducing or moving a subject

An effective move is to insert a subject if a sentence is lacking one or to move a subject to the beginning of a sentence. For example:

Passive: The duet was sung by Mary and Joe.
Active: Mary and Joe sang the duet.

Passive: The arrows were loosed.
Active: The archers loosed their arrows.

IV. Tell Me and I'll Forget: Showing Instead of Telling

"Tell me, and I'll forget. Show me, and you'll involve me."

Sol Stein, *Stein on Writing*

In *Stein on Writing*, Sol Stein provides a very helpful guide on one of the rules disliked by many writers: showing the story instead of telling it.

We've moved into a visual age with the likes of TV, film, and Youtube dominating our lives. People enjoy seeing stories unfold, experiencing them, using them as a means to escape from mundanity and to go on adventures their own lives do not allow for. And this is why, as a writer in our contemporary age, showing a story instead of telling it is becoming more important than ever.

Stein, a master editor of some of the most widely-read books in the world, states that a failure to show the story is, in his view, one of the chief reasons for rejecting a manuscript.

Let's begin by taking a look at why this 'rule' has become so unpopular.

The problems with telling

Let's make something clear right off the bat: telling has its place. A writer has and must hold the power to make months and years pass within a single sentence. When it comes to showing instead of telling, there are a few common pitfalls which writers can become trapped in, as outlined by Stein.

1. **Backstory** – telling the reader what's happened before the story begins. Stein is of the view that such information should be shown either in a narrative summary or in a rather controversial flashback. There are other ways of doing this, though, as we'll see when we look at world-building.

2. **Telling what a character looks like.** This is a tricky one. Instead of just saying, for example, a character is tall, Stein recommends trying to show it with imagery. "He had to stoop under every doorway" to illustrate a man's height, for instance.

3. **Telling what a character sees, hears, smells, touches, tastes, and feels** emotionally. We'll go into more detail with this below, particularly in the next chapter when we consider sensory writing.

Let's break these down further with some examples.

"Henry, your son the doctor is at the door."

This sentence is a great example of the problems with telling. Can you see how forced it seems, the detail of Henry's son being a doctor shoved down our gullets? See what you think of this version:

"Do you think Harold would look more like a doctor if he grew a beard?"

Now, this is better. We can picture Henry's clean-shaven son and the fact that he's a doctor has been shown to us in a more subtle and interesting way.

This is what Stein is getting at in pitfall number two above—showing the details of our characters rather than just telling us about them. When we see a tall person enter a room, we watch them stoop to get through a doorway, or how they bend their necks to talk to others. In describing these details and acts we get a much more vivid image in our minds in comparison to a description of them just being 'tall'.

This leads us to one of the key positives in favour of showing instead of telling: characterisation. What can we reveal to the reader about our characters without telling them anything? Let's look at one of Stein's examples of a woman who loves her children dearly:

> *"Helen was a wonderful woman, always concerned about her children."*

Very 'tell-y'. It's a bland description, devoid of imagery. See what you think of this version:

> *"When Helen drove her children to school she insisted on parking up and with one in each hand, accompanied them to the door."*

Here we're shown a clear image of how much Helen loves her children. This one sentence reveals how much she cares without any mention of the word 'cares' or 'loves'. We can picture her walking them right up to the door, kissing them goodbye and embracing them as if she never wanted to let go. At the same time, it leaves the reader scope to ask questions which in turn draws them deeper into the tale. Why does Helen care so much? Are her children under some kind of threat? Is Helen too loving? Will she ever let her children grow up? And now we're engaged with the story.

Let's take a look at number three on Stein's list of traps: emotions.

"Neil felt anxious."

How about this?

"Every sound Neil heard, even the slightest scuff, caused him to look back and peer into the gloom."

Saying someone is anxious is easy. Showing it is a skill. This specificity allows a reader to connect with the character, draws them deeper into the story and creates empathetic ties.

Stein provides another excellent example, which he takes from Pulitzer prize-winner, John Updike. Instead of merely saying his character, Polly, loves swimming, Updike, with eloquence, says:

"With clumsy jubilance, Polly hurtled her body from the rattling board and surfaced grinning through the kelp of her own hair."

Here we see that Polly is grinning as she surfaces, and coupled with her clumsy jubilance, we get the impression that

Polly is in love with what she's doing. See how it creates opportunities for imagery too with that fine piece of description at the end: 'the kelp of her own hair'.

It's easy for someone to sit there and tell the writer to dig deep into all these complex human emotions, unpack them and attempt to describe things that sometimes can only be felt. It's a hard thing to do, and at times emotionally challenging. A starting point is to consider yourself. Have you felt any similar emotions as your characters? Have you experienced any similar situations? How did you react? How did you feel? It's all about seeking to get as close to the mindset of the character as possible.

Nervousness is a good example. When I feel nervous I tend to bite my nails or fidget and my palms become clammy. Instead of just saying a character is nervous, why not show these physical reactions? Let the reader conclude they're nervous. Let them learn about how this character reacts to their feelings.

And this leads us to Stein's first trap: backstory. The temptation exists for a writer to bring the reader up to speed on everything that happened before the story actually begins. You may also know this approach as the info-dump, that is, the dumping of information within the story, sometimes contained in epic prologues. Other times a writer shoves information and detail about characters without taking the time to weave them into the tale. We've seen it in an example above, "Henry, your son the doctor is at the door".

As we'll see in the chapter on world-building, a more of a showing approach is to allow them details to naturally fall into the story as the plot develops and characters are revealed. Trust the reader to join the dots. Give them the challenge.

A show v. tell checklist

Stein provides a helpful little checklist of questions you can ask yourself to see if what you're writing is showing instead of telling:

1. Are you allowing the reader to see what's going on?
2. Does your author's voice stray into the narrative at any point? If so, can you silence that voice with action? It's through telling that the author's voice intrudes.
3. Are you naming emotions instead of conveying them by actions?
4. Is any character telling another something they already know?

This sounds like I should never, ever tell...

Telling has its place. It's particularly useful when trying to move the story forward, and again when it comes to shorter forms of fiction, such as short stories and flash and micro fiction. It's all a matter of necessity. Do you need to progress the story quickly or brush over details? Does this emotion need to be reiterated? Have I spent too much time showing things and now I just need to progress?

Always remember that none of these so-called rules are binding. There's no right way to do this writing gig. Focus on doing it your way.

V. Sensory Writing

Describing how something looks or sounds isn't always enough to bring a story to life. Many people experience things through smells, touch, and taste. In fact, these oft-forgotten senses are some of the most powerful forms of description, things which can enrich a story and give it life.

Let's look at each of the five senses in turn, and then go over some ways to get into the habit of using them.

Sight

One of the 'base' forms of description. Images form in our minds, we describe things we've witnessed or experienced and we transfer them onto the page. Yet it's not as straightforward as it seems.

It would be nigh impossible to describe every aspect of a scene, and even if you did achieve it, nigh impossible to read. Some of the most acclaimed writers, Dickens, in particular, approached it by picking the *right* details. The little things that tell us everything. Let's look at an example from *Great Expectations*:

> "There was a bookcase in the room; I saw, from the backs of the books, that they were about evidence, criminal law, criminal biography, trials, acts of parliament, and such things. The furniture was all very solid and good, like his watch-chain. It had an official look, however, and there was nothing

merely ornamental to be seen. In a corner, was a little table of papers with a shaded lamp: so he seemed to bring the office home with him in that respect too, and to wheel it out of an evening and fall to work."

This is Jagger's office. Though he doesn't feature, we've gleaned much about who he is from details like the types of books upon the shelves and the paper-filled table, suggesting he lives a busy, professional life.

Colour is another fantastic tool when it comes to sight. Dickens was known for using colours to portray emotions or themes, such as red for frustration or anger, black for death, white for purity or goodness. Using colour, particularly with themes, can add extra layers to a story.

Sound

Something I learned not so long ago is that ducks don't quack. They tend to grunt or even cackle. It's easy to assume how things sound, but sometimes what we assume is wrong. It's always worth taking time to research. In doing so you may find new and original ways to describe the sound. Using metaphors and similes, particularly if the sound is unusual, is a great way to bring clarity to descriptions.

Another often overlooked thing is silence. Silence is an excellent tool to set the tone or build an atmosphere. A noiseless forest. A still, foggy street. Eerie.

Description of sound is also underused when it comes to people's voices. Nobody sounds the same, and a person's voice makes such a difference to how we form views of them.

Touch

Touch is, in my view, one of the most powerful yet underrated senses, particularly in writing, and if you can convey it in an effective way, you'll reap the rewards.

The scope of this sense depends on the nature of the scene, but imagine, for example, walking barefoot through a forest. The softness of moss between your toes, the cool slime of mud, the pokes and scratches of sticks and stones. Such details can draw readers deeper into the story.

As a brief exercise, close your eyes and pick something up. Describe how that object feels. What features does it have? The texture? Sturdiness? Width? Weight?

Taste

Taste is one of the more neglected senses—the one that sits in the corner, out of sight and mind. Like all of the senses, taste can enrich your tale. How many times have you said the phrase, "It tastes like ...". Your characters, more than likely, have experienced such things too.

Like smell, taste can serve as a trigger for memories. For example, a husband who shared a love for apple turnovers baked by his deceased wife is reminded of her whenever he eats one. It can also trigger emotions. There've been times when I've eaten food that tasted so good I bounced with glee in my chair.

Smell

We, at last, arrive at smell, though its place is no reflection on its importance. The power of smells cannot be underestimated. We smell things all of the time and those smells help to shape our impressions. What can you smell right now?

A smell helps us to form a judgement on things, such as whether something's okay to eat. And crucially, smells can trigger vivid memories and emotions, vital tools to any writer. Take for example the smell of marihuana and how that can incite fear in some people, yet in others provokes memories of happiness and peace.

Here's an example from James Joyce's *Ulysses* of how smells (and tastes) can enrich prose.

> "*Mr Leopold Bloom ate with relish the inner organs of beasts and fowls. He liked thick giblet soup, nutty gizzards, a stuffed roast heart, liverslices fried with crustcrumbs, fried hencods' roes. Most of all he liked grilled mutton kidneys which gave to his palate a fine tang of faintly scented urine.*"

Using the senses as a checklist

Something I've sought to do to improve my sensory writing is to include the five senses within the planning process. It's good to save it until the end when you've plotted out your story or chapter.

What I do is read over the plan and try and place myself in the scenes. Working my way through each sense, I list everything that pops into my head.

1. **Sights.** It'll be unlikely that you need to spend too much time on sight, but taking the time to consider things in detail can

provoke new and unique ideas. What little details can be included? Remember the power of specificity.

2. **Sounds.** Next, onto sounds. Like sights, it's unlikely you'll need to spend too much time on this but it's always helpful to consider the likes of character's voices and any usual sounds that could be featured.

3. **Smells.** When it comes to smells a good starting point is to list everything that comes to mind, even mere whiffs, which can be the most telling of all. Smells can provoke memories and emotions too, like the smell of perfume could remind a character of their dead lover, and that leaves you open to describe emotions.

4. **Touch.** What can your character touch or feel? How does the hilt of the sword feel in your character's fingers? How does the touch of a vivacious woman feel to your lonely character? What information can be gleaned from the manner of a handshake?

5. **Taste.** Lastly, what tastes, if any, can you include? Is your character eating? Can they taste blood after being punched in the cheek? Do they enter a room where the smell is so foetid they can taste it?

Exercises

Here are a few useful exercises to get into the swing of using the senses. The more you practice, the more it'll become ingrained in the way you write.

- **One place, one sense.** As the title suggests, think of a place and describe everything you can using just one sense.

Challenge yourself. Pick a sense you feel you struggle with. Or do one sense, then a different one.

- **Walk and write**. Take a notepad and write five headings: sight, sound, touch, taste, smell. The next time you go out, even if it's just to the shop on the corner, write down everything you experience. The touch of the rain or breeze, how the pavement feels underfoot, snippets of passing conversation you hear, the whistle of birds, how that warm and crispy sausage roll tastes. *Warning* You may look odd stopping all the time.

- **Close your eyes and pick something up.** This one was mentioned above, but it's a powerful tool. Jot down everything you can think of.

- **Pick your favourite food and eat!** This one's a bit more fun. Take chocolate for example. Savour each bite and write down everything, from taste to texture, the sounds of it breaking in your mouth, and importantly, how it makes you feel.

Writing Fight Scenes

I often see people asking about writing fight scenes and the guidance on it is pretty scant, so in this chapter, with axes in hand, I thought we'd battle our way through a quick guide.

There seem to be a few general rules of thumb for writing fight scenes. They are:

- Blow by blow is boring;
- Clarity is king;
- Show instead of tell.

Let's look at each in detail.

Blow by blow is boring

"He swung left, then right, dodged a lunging blow from behind, rolled to the right, raised his sword to parry another attack."

Bestselling fantasy writer Brandon Sanderson is of the view that a fight scene should not be a stream of blow after blow until everyone's dead. Rather, it ought to be a portrayal of a character's physical and mental state as they experience danger and react to conflicts.

In movies seeing every punch and kick, decapitation or shooting is sadistically entertaining. On the page, it's a different story. It can slow down the pace and make for confusing, hard to follow passages which serve to frustrate the reader, make them skip the scene or worse, close the book.

This isn't to say that blow by blow should be avoided. Used in the right way, it can reveal a character's skills or flaws. A good balance, it seems, is to do a bit of blow by blow, and then a bit of description, or if writing in the first person or third person limited perspectives, some thought or emotional reflection.

For a good example of a complex battle scene, I recommend Helms Deep in book two of *The Lord of the Rings*. Considering how epic the film version is you'd expect it to be a pretty big chapter. In fact, at twenty pages it's relatively short.

Clarity is king

Battles are frantic affairs. Walls of bodies crashing together, horses charging and rearing, arrows darting in all directions... If there's no clear narrative of what's happening, there's a good chance the reader will throw the book against the wall. The reason? They want to know what happens but the words won't tell them. There are a few things you can do to achieve clarity.

If you're writing about a large battle, it helps to **map it out**, particularly if there are structures, cities or towns involved. By **mapping**, you reduce the risk of contradicting yourself, and crucially, reduce the risk of the reader becoming confused. You'll also have a much clearer picture in mind of what's going on and where, allowing you to write with a stronger, more confident voice; a crucial thing when it comes to writing scenes of such significance.

With so many graphic and vivid scenes it can be easy to over-do the description. **Consider using simpler language**. The reader just wants to see what happens. Battles are exciting for readers; the writer's job is to guide them through it to the end without confusion.

Another thing to consider is use of passive voice. Battles by their nature are action-packed so it makes sense to ditch the passive voice and **use the active**.

Consider using shorter sentences. A short sentence increases the pace, whereas medium and long sentences temper it. It's harder to get lost in a shorter sentence too, making for an easy, fluid read.

Be specific. Name locations, individuals, weapons. It provides all important clarity; we're not wasting time working out who's who.

Showing instead of telling

It's easy to fall into the trap of talking about fight scenes rather than actually showing them. We've been over the benefits of showing a story rather than telling it, so we won't repeat it here.

Something film and TV lacks is the ability to show the viewer how a character is feeling. Battles and wars are chaotic and brutal and those involved experience horrific, life-altering things. The power of writing lies in exploring that. How would you feel as you stood on the walls of a keep as thousands of orcs charge toward you? How would it feel to swing a sword and cut through flesh and bone? Perhaps your character is indifferent to death and fear, even thrives on them.

There are ways for you to do more showing and less telling:

- Use the five senses.
- Make connections between characters and the events unfolding around them, such as helping a comrade who's about to be gutted, or targeting a specific enemy across the battlefield.
- Make the character use resources around them in interesting ways. Perhaps they use a ballista to disrupt the charge of an onrushing foe. I always think of Legolas and how he used a charging oliphaunt to take out another.
- If you're writing a large battle scene in which you wish to cover a lot, you could use numerous perspectives to reveal how things are developing across the battlefield. It gives a variety of emotion and perspective too, enriching the tale.
- You can use italics for introspective thought. I first came across this in George R.R. Martin's writing, and a lot of other authors use it too. It's an excellent way to get closer to a character, and a great way of getting around just telling the reader what emotions a character is feeling.

Break moulds

It's easy to get sucked into the ideas we're familiar with, such as those we see on the screen or read about in the history books. The great thing about writing and crafting your own tales is the unlimited possibilities. You could write about a single battle involving a million people, or the siege of a giant fortress, like in David Gemmell's *Legend.* Think of interesting and different places fights or battles could take place. Let your mind run wild.

Tone

Bear in mind the tone you wish to set. Is this fight going to be one of desperation? Anger? Helplessness? This is a very important influence as to how you write the fight, particularly in the emotional reactions of your characters and how it all pans out.

Lifelike?

It helps to make a decision at the outset as to how lifelike you wish your fighting to be. In medieval times if armed with a sword and shield a soldier held up their shield while swinging wildly over the top or side, all the while bashing forwards to try and push the enemy line back or break it altogether. There was no graceful swordsmanship in such bloody warfare. Survival by any means was everything.

It helps to take the time to learn how weapons work. Assume nothing. Visit museums, historical sites like castles and keeps, even do a few archery or sword fighting lessons. Quite a few authors do, and I have myself. It'll give you crucial experience and knowledge, allowing you to write with more depth and conviction.

Battles don't have to be lifelike, though. It could be like *L.O.T.R.* where highly competent characters cleave their way through entire armies. If you do go down this route, it helps to maintain consistency to avoid annoying the reader.

World-Building

I. Playing Creator

"I propose to speak about fairy-stories, though I am aware that this is a rash adventure. Faërie is a perilous land, and in it are pitfalls for the unwary and dungeons for the overbold."

J.R.R. Tolkien

The world in which a story is set is important to any tale, particularly when it comes to fantasy. We read these kinds of stories to escape to new and unexplored worlds filled with possibilities, mysteries, and oddities. This chapter explores a few tools to help you build a world from scratch.

How do you build an entire world?

Let's just say it's going to take a little longer than seven days.

It's easy to become caught up in the world-building process. For some, it consumes all of their attention, to the extent that they do a Tolkien and for years do nothing but detail everything down to the smells of each made-up flower. For others the world is a stage upon which the story takes place, with the world immediately around the characters the only parts that are revealed, an approach we'll look at in more detail in the chapter that follows.

Generally, a story takes place either in the world we know and live in, or an entirely fictitious world, known as a 'secondary world.' As the focus here is on fantasy, it's the creation of the latter we'll explore.

Sanderson's approach

Brandon Sanderson has his own approach to building a secondary world which focuses on two things: **physical settings** and **cultural settings.**

Physical settings

Physical settings encompass the things that exist if humans—or whatever species your characters are—did not exist. So for example the terrain, flora, fauna, weather, cosmology, geology, laws of physics.

In one of Sanderson's own books, *Mistborn: The Final Empire*, the world is plagued by ash falls and dense mists which descend each night. Consider too Terry Pratchett and his *Discworld* books, which involves a world constructed on the back of a giant turtle floating through space. If you're struggling to think of things, experiment with removing yourself from the physical world. What if the sky was green and the grass blue? For designing a world with oceans, rivers, mountains, swamplands, deserts and the like, look at my chapter on cartography in Part Two.

Cultural settings

This covers things influenced by man, or things that can be physically manipulated or changed, such as laws, politics, religion, government, language, structures, landmarks, philosophies, foods, music, fashion, folklore, weapons, technology, clothing, histories, rights, jobs, medicines ... the list could go on.

It would be impossible to write a book of readable length if you covered every one of these things, and these are but a handful. The trick, it seems, is to pick a few and explore those in detail, perhaps bringing in other related settings in less detail.

The point is to channel your world-building into these settings, which in turn will open up doors to other aspects of the world. Piece by piece you're revealing all those wonderful details you spent weeks and months conjuring.

George R.R. Martin is an expert when it comes to this approach. He writes his own songs and poems, goes into great detail about the food the characters eat, like the 'bowl of brown' in Flea Bottom. Some of his most iconic scenes are those at feasts and balls with vivid descriptions of songs and meals. It's his use of songs and food that brings in histories and other facts about his world and he does it wonderfully.

If at all possible, Sanderson recommends seeking *conflicts* between the different cultural settings you choose to explore. It cannot be understated how crucial creating conflict is, and if you can intertwine conflict with your world-building you're on the right path. For example, the clash between religion and science and jobs and technology. Having a character that cares passionately about a setting also provides a vehicle for revealing much about it, such as a character that loves to cook, like Talon in Raymond Feist's Riftwar Cycle.

Again, have fun with cultural settings. Let your mind run free. Remove the shackles of reality. Anything is possible in a world of your own creation.

Draw a map

Even if, like me, you have the drawing ability of a goat, it really does help to sketch a map of your world, continent, region or city. Places will become grounded in your mind, giving you a more authoritative voice when you speak about them. It allows you to add crucial specificity, something that will enhance your story no end.

Your map doesn't have to be a work of art. That all comes at the end when the writing is done. A crude outline of things is all you need. I've drawn one on the inside wall of my shed. If you would like to have a go at designing a map, there are a few pieces of software to help, such as https://inkarnate.com/

Ask questions

One way to help conjure a world is to ask questions: who, what, where, when, how. What type of magic exists in the world? How does someone gain the power to use it? Are there different kinds of abilities and spells? Is there a limit as to how much magic one person can use?

Such questions are invaluable. And try not to, as is tempting, to settle for the first thing that pops into your head. Push yourself to think of different options and possibilities. Keep asking 'what if?' And if you can't think of an answer, worry not. Move on. Your subconscious will be working away on that, and one day the answer will, with a bit of luck, come to you. You'll know it when you get it.

Here's a very helpful list of world-building questions courtesy of the Science Fiction and Fantasy Writers of America. http://www.sfwa.org/2009/08/fantasy-worldbuilding-questions/

Explore and research

One of the best ways to come up with ideas for your world is to get out into the *real* world and explore. There's nothing more powerful than actually seeing rolling hills and mountains, walking through forests and fields or busy city streets, hearing the noises of factories, the smells of the beach or a harbour. It allows you to write with experience.

Research is important to gain a greater understanding of how something works. If rivers form a big part of your story, learn how they work, the different types of river, how tributaries and meanders are formed, and so on. Again this gives your voice more authority and gives you the tools to describe things with confidence and conviction.

Build as you go

If you're feeling impatient and don't fancy doing any of the above, by all means, build as you go along. Write your story, see where it takes you. You may reach a point where your character needs to go to a new city. You can then ask yourself questions. How do they get there? What towns do they stop at along the way? What kind of city is it they're going to? A thriving metropolis or a besieged ruin? What's the population size? What's the economy built upon? The downside with this approach is you'll probably have to revert to ensure consistency and to fill in any gaps.

II. Revealing a World

So you have your world, how do you reveal it to your reader?

The Iceberg

The philosophy of the iceberg is to reveal a little of your world while holding back much more, just like with an iceberg we merely see its tip, while beneath the water the bulk of its mass lingers. In essence, we're showing the reader the view through the keyhole, teasing them so they want to beat down the door and see everything else. You may be wondering why go to the effort of all that detail? Through experience, you don't often know which direction your story takes so to have that bank of information ready to use makes those changes a lot easier and fluid.

So how do you achieve this?

- **By dropping hints**. Show a little, then a little more, gradually removing the shroud surrounding your world.
- Brandon Sanderson uses the term **'maid and butler dialogue'**. This means that characters should discuss things they know about, but the reader does not. The reader is something of an observer and it's up to them to learn what they can from the conversation.

- Another way of using dialogue is to drop in references to the wider world. For instance, if your fantasy world is called Nagoya, a character could say: "What in Nagoya are you talking about?"

- Or you could use metaphors or similes with things from your world, like the tallest peak in the land could be named Devil's Rock, and a character could say: "He's as bloody tall as Devil's Rock."

- Another way to reveal details is to **feature a character that's unfamiliar with the world around them.** New sights, smells, sounds. They're exploring with the reader, and then you can reveal the glorious details you long to share, like how each and every bloody flower smells.

- **Try not to info dump!** By this, I mean spewing onto the page every little detail that pops into your head. We're all guilty of it. The reader doesn't want to know the history of a city's sewage system unless it's pertinent to the tale.

- **Watch out for repetition.** When revealing a world it can be easy to labour points or refer to things more than once. Constant editing and critiques from trusted sources can help fix this.

There's a right time to share

One temptation for the writer is to foist upon the reader every detail of backstory before the story actually begins. We've been over this in a previous chapter.

The best way, according to Sanderson, is to be sparse with detail during the first few chapters, keeping the focus on the characters and generating empathy toward them. Reward the reader with little details as you go along, and later on, when everyone's comfortable and engaged with the characters and plot, open the door to the wider world.

Additional tools

Here are a few extras you might fight useful:

- There's a subreddit dedicated entirely to world-building. Here you can post your ideas, discuss possibilities and get all important feedback.
  https://www.reddit.com/r/worldbuilding/
- An article by author Tad Williams on world-building
  http://www.fantasyliterature.com/thoughtful-thursday/thoughtful-thursday-tad-williams-talks-about-world-building/
- A webinar on world-building with the editor of 'The Martian', Michael Rowley.:
  https://blog.reedsy.com/live/worldbuilding-tips-editor-martian/

III. A Minimalist Approach

Not long ago I took part in a Reddit Ask Me Anything session (AMA) and somebody put this statement to me:

> "*Modern fantasy seeks smallness, in view, in scope, in characters. Readers want a quick twenty-page epic, preferably in a single house.*"

That made me wonder. And panic too. Do readers want small worlds now? What about all this time and effort I've invested creating this world?

Before I go any further, a clarification point. A minimalistic approach refers to the level at which you reveal your world. You still have to world-build, you're just giving the reader a peep-hole view, showing them what is necessary for the purposes of the story.

I looked into this approach some more and came across Patrick Rothfuss who has much to say on the matter. Here's a passage from an article of his:

> "*But when you're writing fantasy, especially secondary-world fantasy (By which I mean fantasy where the story takes place in a world other than our own) the reader doesn't know*

anything about your world. They don't know the cultures, religions, magic, or cities. The reader doesn't know anything about the myths and legends of the world.

Now a lot of times, this is one of the major selling points of the book. A big payoff of secondary-world fantasy is the thrill of exploration. We get to see new countries, fantastic creatures, odd cultures, curious magics, etc etc.

And, honestly, this is one of the big perks of being a fantasy writer. We get to build castles in the sky, then show them off to people.

So here's how it goes wrong.

1. *You create something for your fantasy world: a creature, a culture, a myth, whatever.*

2. *You're proud of your creation. You're excited about it. You love it with a fierce love.*

3. *You need to describe this thing to your reader, because if they don't understand how it works, your story won't make sense.*

    (3b. Remember, the story is the real reason people are there. Story is everything. Story is god.)

4. *So you start to explain how folks in the Shire celebrate their birthdays. (This is important because one of the first major events of the book is a birthday party.) You talk about how hobbits give presents away at their parties instead of receiving them. (This is important because it ties into why Bilbo is going to hand over the ring to Frodo.)*

Then you start talking about how some of these presents get passed back and forth, party after party. And how those items are actually called mathoms, and how there's actually a museum full of mathoms at Michel Delving, which is in the Westfarthing of the shire... You see what happens? It's easy for an author to get so caught up in the details of the world they created, that they go off the rails and give us more than is really necessary for the story..."

This invariably leads us to the notorious info-dump. We've all been guilty of it. Even the greats like Tolkien, though in his defence he wrote in a different era. And I'll be the first to hold my hand up. The first draft of my first chapter was 12,000 words long and most of those words were dreary passages of info-dumping.

Perhaps this is where this minimalistic approach has come from, as a backlash against authors indulging too much in world-building, in info-dumping their readers' poor brains to bits. I've been reading a lot of upcoming authors of late, helping them with reviews and edits, and it's a persistent problem I encounter. One book I recently read had a prologue setting out the history of the world and story, then in chapter 1 the story began and I was somewhat engaged. Then came chapter 2 and another massive info-dump. It lost me.

Are readers getting fed up with big, epic worlds?

Maybe. I think it all depends on the type of story you're trying to tell and the type of reader you're looking to attract. In a high fantasy story, for example, some degree of world-building is inevitable as characters quest to save the world or whatever. In newer types of fantasy, such as contemporary or urban, the focus seems to be less on the world and more on characters and plot.

I don't think it's something we can just dismiss as a trend though. Rather it ought to be regarded as a warning that readers are getting fed up with being info-dumped, that more time, care, and ingenuity needs to be invested when it comes to showing our worlds.

So what do we writers do? As Rothfuss said:

> "What makes this such a horrible problem is that "too much" is largely a matter of taste. Some readers really *do* want to read all the details of the ancient Shi-Ang dynasty, and how their government relied upon the use of telepathy crystals. Other readers just want you to hurry up and get to the part where the Lesbian Unicorn Sisterhood initiates apprentice Ayllisia into the secrets of the Eternal Kiss.
>
> It's also a matter of style. Some writers are better at making exposition engaging than others. Some worlds are more alien than others, requiring more explanation.
>
> My personal philosophy is to err on the side of caution. Given the choice, I'd prefer to give too little description and leave you wanting more, rather than give a lot and risk you being bored."

Don't you just hate it when there's no straightforward answer? All you can do is bear in mind the advice like

Rothfuss's, as well as the helpful techniques such as 'the iceberg.'

It boils down to the story you're trying to tell and what the reader expects from that type of story. But be warned: the days of the info-dump, it seems, are over.

A Guide to Story Lengths

This chapter looks at the lengths of fiction in its various forms: micro, flash, short, novelettes, novellas, and novels. But it begins with a few words of caution: **forget word counts.**

"A story is as long as it needs to be."

This was the best bit of advice I received when querying how long my first novel should be. Writing the first draft of any story with a word count in mind can be stifling. At that stage of the process, you require unlimited creative freedom. You want to see where your characters take you and how the plot develops. A tight word count may dissuade you from exploring those detours, which may harm your story.

Then again, some of you may find that a helpful thing, a tool to keep you focused. With my second novel, the publisher set a limit of 100,000 words. I didn't like the impingement at first, but it helped to keep my writing on track and, hopefully, encouraged precision. It all boils down to a matter of perspective and what works for you.

Why do word counts matter at all? If you write a book 500,000 words long, few if anyone is going to read it unless you've got the reputation of George R.R. Martin. Weighty bastards are a hard sell. You're asking someone to invest their precious time in your book, and publishers know that. So if you want to get a look-in, you need to be aware of industry standard word limits. Let's explore further.

Micro and flash fiction

As the name suggests, the word limit of **micro fiction** is small, around 100 words, sometimes 150 depending on the publisher. Perhaps the most famous example of micro fiction is Hemingway's "For sale: baby shoes. Never worn." It's becoming an increasingly popular medium, so it's worth having a stab at it.

The limit for **flash fiction** is a bit more gracious, between 1,000 and 1,500 words but could be as low as 500 or 750. It depends on the publisher. It's similar to micro fiction in that it's a hard format to master, but again, it's popular, with most stories read in no more than a few minutes.

Short stories

Short stories come in a range of lengths, usually up to around 7-8,000 words, but can be as many as 17,500 (though as we'll see below this strays into the realm of novelettes). Since I have a fair bit of data at my disposal from compiling a list of short fiction publishers, I thought I'd do a bit of maths.

The average word limit using the range in the table toward the end of this book is 7,500 words, which tends to be the limit set by most publishers. The most common word count limit is 5,000. With 7,500 words being the average limit. Again, preferences vary between publishers. Some like their short fiction short—if paying by the word it's cheaper, and some have a set number of pages to fill in anthologies and journals.

Novelettes and novellas

A **novelette** isn't quite a short story and isn't quite a novella, usually lingering in the range of between 7,500 to 20,000 words. It's for the short stories that you couldn't stop writing. A word of warning: they can be hard to get published. Too long for a magazine, too short for a book. You may find a collection of three or four novelettes together.

A **novella** is a thicker tome and lies in the realm of around 20,000 to 50,000 words, sometimes as many as 70-75,000. There are many dedicated publishers of novellas, and publishers of shorter fiction sometimes open their gates to stories of novella length.

An intriguing trend I've noticed from my list of publishers of longer fiction is that many publishers set their minimum, usually around 10-20,000 words, and do not specify the limit. This suggests you've got a fair bit of freedom when it comes to finding a publisher for novellas.

Novels

The length of novels can range from around 70,000 words up to 150,000, or even more. The limit is dependent on the publisher, genre and your own stature as a writer. YA novels, for instance, tend to be around the 80,000-word mark, with fantasy's (depending on the sub-genre) around 120,000-130,000.

The industry recommended length for a debut novel is around 80,000 to 120,000 words. In the eyes of the publishing world, you're untested; a reader may not take a chance on an unknown author with a wordy book. Saying that, some of the longer debuts in the genre have smashed that limit. Raymond Feist's *The Magician* is 315,085 words long and *The Eye of the World*, book one in Robert Jordan's The Wheel of Time series, is 261,290 words long. If a novel is good enough, it will be published.

All this information may be fine and well, but what if you're going down the self-publishing route?

Word counts and self-publishing

When it comes to self-publishing your work, you are the master. You can set your own word limit if you set one at all. This is perhaps one of the best things about this option.

While having unlimited freedoms, it's worth keeping the industry standards in mind. The publishing industry knows the lengths readers prefer—it's their job after all. When it comes to your own piece, a hefty word length may dissuade potential buyers. Consider also other aspects. If you've got a 1,000 page book, how much is that going to cost to print? Do self-publishing outlets even print books so voluminous? Other factors may dictate what you can and cannot do.

An Approach to Editing

I've recently begun the process of editing the hideous mess that is my first work in progress and soon became ensnared like Frodo in Shelob's Lair. As Frodo probably asked himself during that hairy predicament, *"There must be an easier way of doing this."*

Using everything I've learned to date about editing, I decided to put together a process, or rather an approach, to editing a story. As with most things when it comes to writing, this is something that works for me, and chances are, it may not work for you. But if nothing else it's an example, one that you may use to build your very own system.

An approach to editing

A good story is grown. It takes weeks, months, even years of careful nurturing, uncovering the meanings hidden within, fixing characters so they leap from the page, refining plot and prose to make it gripping and immersive. Just like growing a plant, a story requires patience and dedication.

There is no exact science when it comes to editing. Some writers edit as they go along, ensuring each page is in tip-top shape before moving on. Others bash out the first draft and then pick it apart. Some don't bother at all. The method below is one

I've found particularly useful. It's tailored more toward short story writing but could apply to chapters in novels too.

1. After a day or so, undertake a re-read of the first draft, correcting any glaring errors which leap off the page to ensure readability. Refrain from getting drawn into editing challenges, but by all means, highlight them for later attention.

2. Set the story aside for a few weeks. The longer the better.

3. Go through it once more, this time attending to major matters—the core elements of a story—plot, character, theme and dialogue. Master editor, Sol Stein, recommended this approach, and it makes sense. Think of it like fixing a car. You wouldn't start with the window wipers if the engine's fucked. Set about correcting any issues which fall under these umbrellas. They're usually the hardest and trickiest to resolve.

4. Major matters considered and re-worked, now read over it once more, pruning the new sections you may have added. Remember, new additions will be in first draft form so will need attention later on. Consider and fix problems with prose too. Under the umbrella of prose, I'd include everything from grammar, syntax, structure, adjectives and adverbs, passive voice, sensory language, showing instead of telling and revealing the wider world.

5. Send it to people to read. Ask friends and family, though people you do not know is always the more effective;

they're more likely to be honest with their views. If you're struggling to find people to read your work, try the following groups:

Fantasy Writers Support Group (Facebook)
Writing Bad (Facebook)
The Sci-Fi and Fantasy Writing Collective (Facebook)
Writer's Tips and Feedback (Facebook)
Writers Helping Writers (Facebook)
www.reddit.com/r/FantasyWriters
www.reddit.com/r/Fantasy

If you have a mailing list, ask them. Some of the best advice I've received has come from my subscribers in response to my requests for fresh eyes. When you send out your story, ask for their views on the major components above all else: character, plot, theme, dialogue and prose.

6. After a few weeks, re-read the story with the comments of readers in mind. As always, set about correcting major problems before any other. If a number of people raise the same issues, then you know you ought to fix them. If readers raise a number of different issues, take time to consider them before going ahead and changing—their complaints may be a personal preference.

7. After leaving the story another week or so, revisit. The more times you read through it, the better.

8. This stage is optional, but if you can factor it in, your story will be better for it. Send it to readers again. New

readers, if possible. Ask for comments on the piece as a whole—whether the original problems were corrected well enough, prose... everything. This is near enough your final draft.

9. Make any suggested corrections (that you agree with), read over it a couple of times more and then look to get it published.

I hope this helps you in some way. Like I said before, this approach is one that works for me. The more time you spend editing the more you'll come to learn your own preferences and methods. Impatience places the temptation to skip on editing at our feet. Resist it at every turn. For me, editing is where the real writing takes place, the refinement of your crude creation. As a smith polishes his weapons and armour, so must the writer polish his sentences and paragraphs. The more time and effort you invest in it, the better your story will be.

A few other helpful editing tips

Kill your darlings

> *"Kill your darlings, kill your darlings, even when it breaks your egocentric little scribbler's heart, kill your darlings."*
> Stephen King

You've almost certainly heard this before. What does it mean?

You've written something you absolutely love—a beautiful sentence or passage of prose, a vivid description of a person or place—but it doesn't work. Your reader doesn't get it. It doesn't fit with the rest of the story. It has to be killed, banished. You must be as ruthless as Napoleon, but you needn't incinerate those pretty little gems. Save them in a word doc or scrapbook; they'll find their place eventually.

The opening line, paragraph and page

With the opening line, paragraph and page, you either win your reader or lose them. A story needs a good hook, something which grabs the reader, provokes intrigue and makes them *ask questions*. In Raymond Carver's short story, *Why Don't You Dance?* the piece opens with this:

> *"In the kitchen, he poured another drink and looked at the bedroom suite in his front yard."*

Why is there a bedroom suite in his front yard? What kind of drink is he pouring? Alcoholic? Why? From the off, we're asking questions, and we want to know more.

Another way to create intrigue is with dialogue. When writing dialogue it helps to forget about the reader altogether, to try and live in the minds of the characters. They're having their own conversation, the contents and backstory of which they know. It can be more intriguing for the reader to act as a fly on the wall, to encourage them to think about what's being said, and again to make them ask questions.

Spend time on your opening paragraph, heck your opening page. It's by far the most important of all. It's your one shot to win your reader over, to bind them to your story.

Put it away

> "How long you let your book rest ... is entirely up to you, but I think it should be a minimum of six weeks. During this time your manuscript will be safely shut away in a desk drawer, ageing and (one hopes) mellowing. Your thoughts will turn to it frequently, and you'll likely be tempted a dozen times or more to take it out ... Resist temptation ... When it comes to the correct evening ... take your manuscript out of the drawer. If it looks like an alien relic bought at a junk-shop or yard sale where you can hardly remember stopping, you're ready."
>
> Stephen King, On Writing.

The point of King's advice is to allow your mind to forget about your story altogether, so when it comes to that first revision, you're coming at it with fresh eyes.

You'll notice spelling mistakes and inconsistencies, holes in the plot or jarring bits of dialogue or prose; new ideas that may have been stewing in your mind will come to the fore; you'll see areas lacking description, or notice over-description and info-dumping. With fresh eyes, you can see and tackle all of these problems.

A few books on editing

Here are a few helpful books on editing:

Stein On Writing, Sol Stein

The First Five Pages, Noah Lukeman

On Writing, Stephen King

The Elements of Style, William Strunk Jr.

The Art of Fiction, John Gardner

The Art of Dramatic Writing, Lajos Egri

Knowing When to Re-write

I had a sickening moment not long ago. While thinking how best to put the pieces of a story together I realised none of it worked. Like trying to place triangles into oblongs. Before nausea came panic, and when at last they both settled, I realised I had a decision to make. Turn back and right the wrongs, or scribble on in ignorance?

In my heart and mind, I knew the changes would make the story better. But to do so would mean significant work. Butchering chapters I was pleased with, removing passages I liked. The hours spent thinking and planning all wasted.

I went on, each word written with less conviction and the urge to go back gnawing at me like an insatiable rat.

I caved. And I'm glad of it.

Being faced with the realisation that something you've invested so much time and effort into isn't good enough, or doesn't work, is one of the hardest things for a writer to endure. I've spoken to writers who forever spend their time re-writing until they get it just right. I've spoken to others who reject the idea. I've spoken to more who aren't sure if it's the right thing to do or not.

In the end, I think it comes down to a gut feeling. When I was struck by this dilemma of either writing on or going back, the idea of re-writing felt like the right thing to do, as much as I loathed it. The newer version excited me. It felt as if I'd unlocked a door leading to the way out of this labyrinthine story writing puzzle.

But when all you have for counsel is yourself, you can never be sure if it's the right thing to do. What if the original version is better? What if I've made it worse? There are, however, some things we can do to help make this crucial and difficult decision a little easier.

Seek the opinions of others

I believe it was Stephen King who said that when approaching feedback on your work, if everybody raises different issues, you can probably ignore them. If they all say the same thing, you need to change it.

In my experience, the areas requiring a re-write have often received comments like, "this is confusing," "this doesn't make sense," "what?", "I don't get this." A bunch of comments like that is a clear sign that things need to change.

Assess the damage

In the first moments when you realise things need to change, despair grips you and makes you want to take that manuscript outside and douse it with lighter fluid.

When I decided I needed to reconsider things, after my initial period of dread I went back and looked back at what actually needed to change. It turned out nowhere near as much as I thought. In fact, out of fourteen chapters, I only needed to change three, and two of them in minor ways. I certainly felt a lot better about re-writing as a result.

It doesn't all have to go

Part of why it's so difficult to come to terms with re-writes is down to the existing content. Blood, sweat and tears have been invested into the crafting of this literary jigsaw. You can't just discard it all and start again.

One thing that works for me is to go through with a highlighter and note the sections I like. It might be entire pages, depending on how precious I'm feeling, or it might be a line or a simile or metaphor. Either way, when it comes to the re-write, you've got the best of your writing on hand to help you out.

If word count's an issue, a re-write will likely fix it

Not so long ago I returned to chapter one of my original work in progress, written about eighteen months beforehand, and was horrified. Twelve thousand words long. What the hell did I write about? I loathe long chapters when reading. How can I not practice what I preach? It had to go.

After I'd finished re-writing the chapter, the word count clocked in at three thousand four hundred. Just over three quarters less. When it came to that second version, I knew what I wanted to say. I liposuctioned the flab and stuck to the point. Now I can say, without a shadow of a doubt, the newer version is better and certainly more readable.

Ask yourself: 'was this my first idea?'

This may just apply to me, but sometimes when mapping out a story I like my first idea so much I settle for it. What I've come to learn is that if I took more time to actually consider other options before deciding on a course then I'd save myself a lot of hardship down the line.

So when I get that first idea that brings so much excitement, I take more time to consider it. You'd be surprised how often that first idea now gets shelved. Try and think of as many possibilities as possible. Unless that initial idea is golden, keep on pondering and jot down every option that comes to mind.

***

Re-writes are neither fun nor are they simple. But when you realise that it has to be done for the sake of the story and characters, it's certainly a sacrifice worth making. For me, one of the worst feelings imaginable would be opening my book and reading through it with regret. So I've come to accept that I'll never get it right the first time, that re-writes are a part of the process. I feel it's helped me grow as a writer. I hope these tips help you too.

Improving Your Craft

Much is learned from life's harsher lessons. When it comes to looking back on previous pieces of writing, we can feel embarrassed or ashamed. Instead, I say look back with pride. Look at it with the knowledge that reading this now you've come to learn what's wrong with it, what its weaknesses are, how you would change it. You know that next time you will do better and appreciate that in recognising all of these things that you have grown and improved as a writer.

Here are a few of the most effective ways I've learned that help me improve my craft.

Read

> *"If you don't have time to read, you don't have the time (or the tools) to write."* **Stephen King.**

Reading helps to teach the very craft of writing. You can learn new words, new perspectives, sentence structure, pacing, characterisation methods, plotting techniques, world-building approaches. You see the 'rules' and how they can be broken.

> *"The most important thing for any aspiring writer, I think, is to* **read***! And not just the sort of thing you're trying to write,*

be that fantasy, SF, comic books, whatever. You need to read
everything. Read fiction, non-fiction, magazines, newspapers.
Read history, historical fiction, biography. Read mystery
novels, fantasy, SF, horror, mainstream, literary classics,
erotica, adventure, satire. Every writer has something to teach
you, for good or ill. (And yes, you can learn from bad books as
well as good ones — what not to do)." **George R.R. Martin**

As well as enjoying (or hating a story) it's important to pay attention to the craft of how it's written, to read analytically. If a particular paragraph has gripped you, take the time to read it again and hone in on what exactly you liked. If you see a word you're unsure of, look up the definition and a few example sentences. Consider as well word usage, syntax, structure, plotting and so on. Imitation is a terrific way to learn.

To get through a few more books, you could try audiobooks. There's a website (and also an app), audiobooks.com, which has few free ones. You've nothing to lose in trying it.

Practice

With everything life has to throw at us it can be hard to find the time and motivation to write. But something is better than nothing. Every word is a step in the right direction.

Take a leaf out of Joanna Cannon's book (excuse the pun). While working as a psychiatric nurse in an underfunded NHS she wrote her debut, bestselling novel, cramming in words before work, after work and during breaks.

But remember, you're practising and improving at the same time. There's no need to pile the pressure on your shoulders of trying to write a game-changing book. Allow yourself the freedom to experiment and explore.

> "The more you write, the better you'll get. But don't write in my universe, or Tolkien's, or the Marvel universe, or the Star Trek universe, or any other borrowed background. Every writer needs to learn to create his own characters, worlds, and settings. Using someone else's world is the lazy way out. If you don't exercise those "literary muscles," you'll never develop them." **George R.R. Martin**

Listen

Lessons linger around every corner, but they must be sought. Everyone knows something you do not and there's no shame in that. Those that succeed listen to those that know more.

Begin with the basics and build from there. Read books on writing, watch or attend lectures, sign up for webinars, courses, workshops. Join forums or writing groups. Discuss, share, critique.

You're learning a new craft, and unless you're James Joyce reincarnate you must take time to learn. Carpenters, electricians, doctors, lawyers go through years of training to master their fields. So must you.

They say it takes 10,000 hours of practice to master something. That's about 90 minutes a day for 20 years. A daunting prospect, but achievable, especially when you work out it's just 10.5 hours per week. Put in the work and trust that everything else will follow.

Experience

The world around us has the power to inspire. Go hiking, walk around your park, even just walk down your street. What do you see that could inspire a novel? A glimpse into the personal life of a stranger? A snippet of overheard dialogue? An unusual building or landmark?

Getting out and seeing the diversity in the appearance of people is a great source for generating ideas for characters. It's remarkable how unique we all look; something I certainly take for granted. And it's the little details that make wonderful stories—scars, tattoos, piercings, hair style, fashion sense—but those details must be found.

Take a pen or paper, or make notes on your phone. Who knows when ideas will pop into your head?

Embrace failure

In failing we learn our weaknesses and better understand ourselves, our motivations and our desires to succeed. It's a necessary part of the process.

Don't let those lows extinguish your desire and enthusiasm. Keep on telling yourself that you *can* write and that you have a story the world must hear. Accept that you're not going to get it right first time, but be determined to keep going until you succeed. When you finally achieve your goal it'll feel better than any drug-induced high.

Keep faith

This one's linked to failing. No matter how down you feel, how ill-motivated you are, how low your confidence may fall, always cling to that flicker of hope.

Savour the little successes, as slight as they may be. A new subscriber to your mailing list, a few lines of feedback in a rejection email, achieving your daily word count, even just writing a word—some days it can be that hard. The world may say no, but the only person who can blow out that hopeful flame is you.

Defeat procrastination

I'll check my emails and 45 minutes later there I am scrolling through Twitter, page still blank. And I hate Twitter.

Remove temptations. Turn off the wifi, leave your phone in another room. Tackle whatever defeats you head on, and be bold in your steps. No half measures. Allow your mind to focus, to forget, to engage. Procrastination is one of the toughest demons of all to overcome, and it's why we'll look at it in a little more detail in our next chapter.

Maintaining Focus

"Until you value yourself, you will not value your time. Until you value your time, you will not do anything with it." M. Scott Peck

Countless hours lost to daydreaming, scrolling through mundanity on the web, reading news articles on subjects I've never shown an interest in. Sometimes I sit there ready to go and a thought pops into my mind. *I've not cleaned the fish tanks in a few weeks.* Another forty minutes go by. Think of all the words that could have been written?

Procrastination is so widely discussed in the writing community I know it's not just me that suffers from this curse. It's in the most frustrating hours that we strive to understand the meaning of things. What is procrastination? Why do we insist on delaying our progression?

You can look at procrastination as having two constituent parts: first, **mental attitude,** and second, **physical distractions**. Attitude is perhaps the most important, distractions being the enabler. So let's first look at what influences our moments of procrastination.

Fear

I think the biggest reason is fear. If we do not try we cannot fail. And in delaying the act of writing we can forever in our minds picture ourselves as successful. Our fantastical dreams live on. We have not tried so we have not failed.

But in not trying we fail. And this is the flaw in the rationale. For years whenever things did not go my way, I recited the saying: "Good things come to those who wait." Comforting, but nonsense. You must act, you must be proactive. Make opportunities for yourself. Be bold and unafraid. Stake your claim, ring fence your piece of the world. And let nobody or nothing halt you in your path.

Well, that's the theory. Reality, as we know, is very different. So what can do to rid ourselves of the curse?

> *"It was my fear of failure that first kept me from attempting the masterwork. Now, I'm beginning what I could have started ten years ago. But I'm happy at least that I didn't wait twenty years."* Paulo Coelho

Turn fear on its head. The very thing we fight every day is, in fact, a powerful source of motivation, maybe the most influential source of all. The greatest motivator for me is the thought of dying and not having finished my scribblings.

> *"Only put off until tomorrow what you are willing to die having left undone."* Pablo Picasso

Forget instant perfection

> *"A primary reason people don't do new things is because they want to do them perfectly − first time. It's completely*

irrational, impractical, not workable – and yet, it's how most people run their lives." Peter McWilliams

Wouldn't it be great if we could write a Hugo award-winning novel first time? No hours spent slaving away over characterisation, plot holes, syntax, adjectives ... Maybe in another universe, but not ours.

The sooner it's accepted that what tends to get written first time around isn't going to be special, the sooner those words are likely to start flowing. Editing is the most significant part of the process. The prospect seems daunting, but the more you learn about the craft, the easier editing becomes, and you may even find yourself enjoying it. So don't beat yourself up while you're writing your first draft. There's ample opportunity to put things right down the line.

Approach writing as if it were a game

My old lawyer job was pretty taxing and dull, so to make things a bit more enjoyable I began to approach it like a game. Tasks and deadlines became challenges instead of problems. Not the kind of game I'd *choose* to play, but choice wasn't a luxury I enjoyed.

You can apply this to writing too. The problems with your manuscript aren't problems but rather challenges to overcome. You can even approach it like an actual game. Write so many words and you get to level 2, 3, 4, and so on. Or look at each word, sentence or paragraph you write as a way of gaining experience points (or XP). It may not work for all of you, but for some, it may be of use.

Reward yourself

In other words, Pavlovian Conditioning—conditioning yourself to write. Think of small rewards you can give yourself. A snack, cup of tea, smoke. Or if you've achieved a lot, a more substantial reward, like a takeaway, a few hours on the PS4, or watching a bit of TV. Anything you enjoy.

In the toughest of times when concentration is waning, you keep on rubbing your eyes, staring anywhere but the page or screen, your reward is there to keep you focused and driven. And when it comes to the reward you can enjoy it even more knowing you've achieved your goals.

Tackle the toughest challenge first

"Do the hard jobs first. The easy jobs will take care of themselves." Dale Carnegie

You awake, brush your teeth, shower, eat a banana, and now you're ready for the world. Resist the temptation to pick those easier jobs first. As Mr Carnegie says, they'll take care of themselves in time. Roll up your sleeves and dive head first into that bastard bit of editing that's been breathing down your neck.

They say you're at your sharpest when you first awake. Maybe so, and if that applies to you, take advantage. The later in the day you leave a big job the more likely you are to postpone it. "No point getting started on that now. I'll do it tomorrow." *Do it now!*

Work in bursts

Getting going is often the hardest part, as users of Viagra can attest to. So take the pressure off your shoulders by making the challenge smaller. Twenty minutes is no big deal. You write a few paragraphs and bang, twenty minutes have gone. But now you've found your flow, you don't want to stop. And next thing you know you've clocked an hour and six hundred words. You've just tricked yourself into productivity.

So those are a few ways to change your thinking. Now it's time to tackle the enablers.

Ditch the smartphones and devices

Most of us have a smartphone, and damn can they be distracting. It's nice to feel connected with our friends, family, and the wider world, but sometimes you need to step away for a few hours, as alien as it feels to disconnect. Leave devices in another room. Lock them in a safe. Get someone in your house to hide them. If you're expecting a call use an old brick of a phone. All you can do on one of them is play 'Snake'.

Establish a writing area

Find your favourite corner of the house, or wherever you like to write, piss all over it and tell everyone else to stay the fuck away. This is your territory now.

Try and free it of distractions. Windows can be good and bad. I love sitting by a window. It can be a great source of inspiration, but also a powerful source of distraction too.

Consider locating your writing space away from where you relax. This is tricky for me because my house is small, which is probably why I prefer writing outside. I'm writing this outside now. It's important to establish this distinction. Writing in bed, for instance, is not a good idea, though bloody comfortable. You associate your relaxing environment with distracting things. Some fellow writers I've spoken to go to cafes, preferably ones without Wi-Fi, which I think is a great idea.

Wind in the web browsing

I'm a sucker for a fail video and browsing through Amazon deals with no intention of buying anything.

Yes, the internet is necessary for research or to look up a word, but there are dictionaries. If you want to keep that Wi-Fi on but still aren't trusting, you can have a look at some of these programs or add-ons for your web browsers:

- *Freedom.* This little app is designed to manage your distractions. You can block websites for specific periods of time. You do however have to pay for it.
- *Self-Control.* Mac only. Like Freedom, it allows you to block websites during specified times. Free.
- *StayFocused.* Add on for Google Chrome. Much the same as the above. Free.
- *LeechBlock.* Add on for Mozilla Firefox. As above. Free.

Try listening to music without lyrics

This may work for some of you, for others not at all. Lyrics are meant to be distracting. I tried this out and found I was a little more focused during instrumental songs. I didn't have any opportunity to bellow out a line, disrupting my flow. I love rock and psych, and classical. Crazy long Allman Brothers jams do it for me, and of course The Lord of the Rings Soundtrack.

Avoid multitasking

Some people pride themselves on their ability to multitask. If you're good at it, nice one. Whenever I try it I can handle it for a while but soon I grow stressed and lose focus on both tasks, meaning nothing gets done. Some of you may be the same. It can be far easier to focus on one task, and in the long run, more efficient.

***

So there are a few weapons to add to your arsenal the next time you go duelling with the devil that is procrastination. I'll leave you with a few motivational quotes, starting with my favourite:

"Words are wind," A Song of Ice and Fire, George R.R. Martin.

"If and When were planted, and Nothing grew." Proverb

"Somebody should tell us, right at the start of our lives, that we are dying. Then we might live life to the limit, every minute of every day. Do it! I say. Whatever you want to do, do it now! There are only so many tomorrows." Michael Landon

"Life, as it is called, is for most of us one long postponement." Henry Miller

Part Two: Writing in the Fantasy Genre

Introduction

I adore the fantasy genre. I can still remember reading *The Hobbit* for the first time back when I was a little 'un and being enraptured by the adventure and possibilities. I grew up during the *Harry Potter* craze and have watched *Game of Thrones* become the most popular TV show of all time (apart from season 8). Fantasy has always been a rich genre, though for too long it has been relegated to a lesser standing. One thing that cannot be denied is its growing popularity, and what phenomenons such as *Potter* and *Thrones* tell us is that people *love* it. They love the escape, the endless possibilities, the curiosities and the intrigues. It's a good time to be writing fantasy. As we'll see, it's a fluid and expanding genre, with dozens of sub-genres branching off it and blending together to create sub-genres of their own.

It's the job of the fantasy writer to create new and original places, people and creatures for people to explore and discover, and in this section, we'll look at how to go about it. We'll look at making maps—always a central tool to the fantasy writer—and what ought to be considered when doing so. The many races found in fantasy will also get a look in and we'll explore whether or not to use the classic race tropes and how to go about finding some originality. And we'll also look at religion and its relationship with fantasy and the possibilities that it offers your tales.

Last of all is a short section on finding inspiration, with a specific look at the Middle Ages—the source of inspiration for *A Song of Ice and Fire, Lord of the Rings* and many other great fantasy books.

By the end, you should hopefully know a bit more about what to expect when it comes to writing in the fantasy genre, as well as being equipped with some useful details to utilise in your own scribblings.

The Many Sub-Genres of Fantasy

The fantasy genre is like a giant oak with great, snaking roots, each one a sub-genre. Some overlap and spawn new sub-genres of their own. Alone, others burrow deeper.

When faced with the prospect of writing a fantasy story or novel, a helpful step is to work out exactly what genre it falls into. For one, you can better target your readers and hone in on their likes and expectations, and two; it helps you aim more precisely at publishers and agents. Here's a rundown on some of the most popular sub-genres.

High Fantasy

A close relation of Epic Fantasy, High Fantasy encapsulates a tale set in a rich, unique and, as is so often the case, a secondary world where magic exists with clearly defined rules. No drugs involved, sorry.

It's arguably the sub-genre most people think of when they hear the term 'fantasy'. *Lord of the Rings* and such. Plots tend to be complex, characters go on epic journeys in which they face many trials and undergo change, not just physically, but mentally too.

This sub-genre has probably influenced every fantasy writer in one way or another, for some encouraging them to go in a different direction, others extracting elements of it and using it in their own way.

Coming of Age, Epic, Sword and Sorcery, Heroic, and many more sub-genres are all linked to High Fantasy.

Examples

The Hobbit, J.R.R. Tolkien

The Name of the Wind, Patrick Rothfuss

The Way of Kings, Brandon Sanderson

The Chronicles of Thomas Covenant. Stephen R. Donaldson

The Demon Cycle series, Peter V. Brett

Epic Fantasy

This is perhaps the most popular sub-genre with stories generally involving a struggle between good and evil spanning several books or series with a significant cast of characters. Epic Fantasy encapsulates gritty, realistic tales as well as those filled with magic, dragons, orcs, or white walkers. The distinction between this sub-genre and High Fantasy lies in the scale of the story, with tales being grander and more expansive, as the name suggests.

Examples

The Lord of the Rings, J.R.R. Tolkien

The Riftwar Cycle, Raymond E. Feist

A Song of Ice and Fire, George R.R. Martin

Chronicles of The Raven, James Barclay

Mistborn, Brandon Sanderson

Wheel of Time, Robert Jordan

Shadows of the Apt, Adrian Tchaikovsky

Urban Fantasy / Contemporary Fantasy

This sub-genre is known by both of the above names. Stories under this umbrella generally take place in the real-world or present-day settings, such as cities. Usually, the fantasy world is hidden amongst the normal one, like in *Harry Potter* or *Narnia*. It's a broad sub-genre, but the key ingredient is magic within a real-world setting.

Examples

Fevre Dream, George R.R. Martin

Harry Potter, J.K. Rowling

Neverwhere, Neil Gaiman

The Chronicles of Narnia, C.S. Lewis

Low Fantasy

In general, the opposite of High Fantasy, though it's title is no reflection on its standing.

Stories can involve a real-world setting, i.e. low on the secondary-world spectrum, with some magical or supernatural features, like with contemporary fantasy. Stories tend to involve a character who discovers this secret, magical world. Stories can also be set in a secondary world but one similar to our own, i.e. no magic or dragons etc.

Low Fantasy stories can be grittier, with more focus on characters, theme and plot than the fantasy world. Common themes explored include social and political upheaval, questionable morals, and flaws in human nature.

Examples

Harry Potter, J.K. Rowling

Neverwhere, Neil Gaiman

Twilight, Stephanie Meyer

Sword and Sorcery / Heroic Fantasy

Both of these sub-genres have their roots in High Fantasy. They tend to involve competent heroes who cut and blast their way to glorious victory. The fact that swords and sorcery tend to feature in both these sub-genres links them closely together. What's the difference then? Heroic fantasy may not feature any magic at all, instead focusing on the grittiness of war and such.

Examples

Chronicles of The Raven, James Barclay

The Lord of the Rings, J.R.R. Tolkien

The Riftwar Cycle, Raymond E. Feist

Legend, Dave Gemmell

Historical Fantasy

Stories of this type tend to be set in our own world but possess one or two fantastical twists, or they can be set in secondary worlds that share some historical similarities to our own, such as medieval life and warfare.

In this sub-genre, there tends to be a balance between realism and fantasy. Plots tend to be more complex and the levels of violence pretty high. Related genres include Steampunk, Alternate History Fantasy, and Celtic Fantasy.

Examples

Abraham Lincoln Vampire Hunter, Seth Grahame-Smith

Jonathan Strange & Mr Norrell, Susanna Clarke

The Falconer, Elizabeth May

Dark Fantasy / Horror

Horror and Dark Fantasy are terms used interchangeably to refer to this sub-genre, though dedicated fans will distinguish between the two. Dark Fantasy tends to focus on creating creepy, intense atmospheres, akin to that of Lovecraft in which he weaves dark and ominous stories into our own world. It can feature fantastical creatures like werewolves, or supernatural elements too. There are few limits when it comes to the weird and terrifying.

Examples

The Dark Tower, Stephen King

Coraline, Neil Gaiman

The Black Company, Glen Cook

Anything by H.P. Lovecraft

Grimdark

Grimdark has its roots in High Fantasy, though over the years has taken a very different path. Featured characters may be anti-heroes or have moral flaws, with the setting being quite grim and gritty, hence the name.

It's certainly one of the more popular sub-genres of late, with writers such as Joe Abercrombie and Anna Smith-Spark two of the more notable writers in the field.

Examples

A Song of Ice and Fire, George R.R. Martin

The Lies of Locke Lamora, Scott Lynch

The Blade Itself, Joe Abercrombie

Empires of Dust, Anna Smith Spark

Steampunk

One of the key characteristics of Steampunk is Victorian-era technologies, such as steam-powered machinery and equipment. Settings range from Victorian England, to completely original secondary worlds, or even the American Wild West.

Magic can feature quite heavily in such stories, with magic and technology often combined or co-existing alongside each other, or even coming into conflict. The detail in such stories tends to be quite high, which is one of the reasons why it's so popular.

Examples

The Anubis Gates, Tim Powers

Perdido Street Station, China Miéville

Shadows of the Apt, Adrian Tchaikovsky

Science Fantasy

This sub-genre sees something of a fusion between Sci-Fi and Fantasy. Technology tends to feature heavily, as does magic. The biggest difference between Sci-Fi and Science Fantasy is the lack of an obligation on the latter to set out the laws of the world according to science, meaning there is a little more leeway when it comes to this particular sub-genre. Settings can be the real-world or secondary world, with the scale often epic.

Examples

The Stone Sky, N. K. Jemisin
Lord of Light, Roger Zelazny
Outlander, Diana Gabaldon

***

What's apparent from this non-exhaustive list is that Fantasy is more of an umbrella term for a whole host of rich sub-genres, some of which are spawning sub-genres of their own. The Fantasy genre is huge. Bigger than any other, I'd say. And it's expanding all the time, which just goes to show how much of a vibrant and popular genre it is.

Further reading

I said at the beginning that the list above is non-exhaustive. You might be reading this thinking your story fits into none of these. Well, there may be other sub-genres or sub-sub-genres which better define it. Checking out some of these other guides may help you out:

http://bestfantasybooks.com/fantasy-genre.php

https://thoughtsonfantasy.com/2015/12/07/17-common-fantasy-sub-genres/?blogsub=confirmed#blog_subscription-5

https://www.worldswithoutend.com/resources_sub-genres.asp

https://editorialdepartment.com/what-the-heck-is-it/

http://marcykennedy.com/2014/04/crash-course-fantasy-sub-genres/

Naming People and Places

I see many questions about naming characters and places, in the fantasy genre in particular. How different should they be? Should they have surnames and grandiose titles? Should I stick an apostrophe in the middle to make it sound more fantasyish?

I've done a bit of research and knocked together a guide to ease those naming woes.

Coming up with names

Let's start with the hard part. I like George R.R. Martin's approach. He takes existing names and gives them a slight twist. John becomes Jon, Edward becomes Eddard, and in what has to be the slightest tweak of all, Jamie becomes Jaime. The point is they're different.

George R.R. Martin also suggests turning to baby books. No doubt he undertakes a similar sort of process, picking names both common and unusual and changing them about if he feels the need. This approach of taking a common name and playing about with it I've found particularly helpful—it strikes a balance between clarity and originality. I simply write down a name, replace letters, remove letters, reorganise, shorten, lengthen. Playing around with vowels is a method I particularly enjoy. For instance, take the name Hal and swap the vowel around—A, E, I, O, U—you can make a different name out of every one.

Another approach is trying online fantasy name generators, and there are shit loads of them. Here's just one: http://www.fantasynamegenerators.com/. I had a browse and this is what I got for elf names:

> Ilrune Zylbanise
>
> Morthil Adrieth
>
> Lhoris Caina
>
> Xhalh Perran
>
> Jhaan Craris
>
> Alosrin Yinwarin
>
> Theodwin Zinmaer
>
> Siirist Heledithas
>
> Alok Pafina
>
> Elorshin Glynralei

Some aren't bad—Alok, Jhaan, Lhoris—but most provide the perfect examples of names that aren't ideal. Too difficult to pronounce. Too wordy. Trying too hard. We'll go into more detail shortly.

One last thing before we move on. When you're set on a name, say it aloud. How does it sound? Then Google it to see if it means something else. Better safe than sorry.

Clarity is king

In fantasy, it's fair to say some names can be a bit crazy. Where did the love for the spontaneous apostrophe materialise?

> "Calt'huun looked at Lym'r, then at Ecka'rd, before at last turning to Pn'agy'my."

I just made that up, but you get the idea. A complex name can draw negative attention, jar the reader's flow and cause headache-provoking frustration if it's too difficult to pronounce.

What do other authors do? Raymond E. Feist called his protagonist in *The Riftwar Saga* Pug. Three letters. Simple. Likewise, Brandon Sanderson in his Mistborn series named his protagonist Vin. George R.R. Martin did the same with Jon and Bran. Nice and simple, no question marks over how it's pronounced.

The names of protagonists and antagonists will feature heavily in your books so avoiding complexity is desirable. Not only that, you'll get fed up of typing it out every time.

The danger of similar sounding names

Linked to clarity, giving characters similar sounding names isn't doing your readers any favours.

In the *A Song of Ice and Fire* books, for instance, Theon's sister is called Asha. Then there's the wildling woman who looks after Rickon Stark called Osha (notice the swapping of the vowels). In the TV series, the decision was made to change Asha to Yara due to the risk of confusion. It people found that confusing the same problem is likely to crop up with one of your own.

Characterising through names

A bland character blends in with the greyness, living briefly in the minds of readers. An eccentric name amid a sea of mundanity can help set a character apart. One way to characterise with a name is to use a surname or title. In David Gemmel's *Legend*, one of the central characters is Druss the Legend. In *Star Wars*, Luke is a pretty dull name, but Skywalker livens it up tremendously.

Think about nicknames too. They can be an effective way to say a lot about a character without having to say anything at all. The Hound or The Mountain from *Game of Thrones* for example.

Characters' age and background

Like in the real world, in fantasy realms names could go out of date. You may have an old man with a name long forgotten amongst the populace. Or the opposite may be true. In our world, we have a shit tonne of John's, James's, David's etc. Your fantasy world could have a whole host of common names too. But always keep clarity in mind. If these characters are central to your story, try and avoid using the same or similar sounding names unless you can give them clear distinguishing features.

A character's background is important too. In your fantasy world people from different regions, kingdoms, countries or continents aren't going to have similar sounding names. It's unlikely someone born in China is going to be called Mark. Again, George R.R. Martin is a believer in this principle. A character from Braavos doesn't have a similar name to someone from Winterfell.

Surnames

They can be underused in fantasy. You may have an orphan character who has no surname, or you could have a monarch with a proud surname rich with tradition and history. Lannister or Stark, for instance. And look at the use of Snow and Sand in *Game of Thrones* and the sway they carry in the story.

Consider adding meanings

A lot of names have meanings behind them such as in African, Arabic and Celtic cultures. African names, in particular, have some beautiful meanings behind them. It's worth doing some research.

The Fantasy Melting Pot

One of the more contemporary complaints about the fantasy genre is its stereotypical races. Elves that live in forests singing to the animals. Beardy dwarves who heft axes bigger than their bodies and defy sadistic dragons for a bit of gold. Orcs that desire one thing and one thing alone: man flesh.

In this chapter I thought we'd look at the three most common races—elves, orcs, and dwarves—explore their classic tropes, and debate whether what we as writers ought to do: re-use, recycle, or rubbish them.

Elves

- About the same height and appearance as humans, though sometimes smaller or taller. They have ears like Spock's with varying pointiness. Usually beautiful to the point of perfection.
- Often found in woods, forests, or tree cities.
- Usually about 10,000,000,000 years old.
- Can come in various sub-races, such as high elves, dark elves, wood elves. High elves tend to be more competent at things such as magic and fighting, an all-around 'superior' being. It's not some kind of stoned elf who's always sniffing flowers and eating shrooms (there's a gap in the market

there). Wood elves are a little more grounded than their 'high' cousins. They're sometimes portrayed as jovial, open-minded folk, and other times as secretive and fiercely protective over their land and kin. Dark elves are the goths and emos of their kin, rejecting the trees and plants and anything happy. They want to corrupt the world with the depressing virus that riddles them.

- Always carries some kind of bow which they can shoot anything with from any distance. Why not shoot three arrows at once while you're at it.

- Can possess some kind of magical ability, such as superior vision, smell or hearing, or a greater handling of magic.

- Very spiritual beings, but with a tradition of fighting. Their warriors seem to have a reluctant air to them like they wouldn't be doing this if it wasn't for the arsehole killing everyone.

- Usually ruled by some semi-divine individual, such as an elder or queen. Elf kings can be quite hard to come by.

- Perhaps a tad racist? They don't care much for dwarves.

Orcs

The word orc comes from an old English word—orcus—which referred to a type of monster or demon, though the Roman God of Death was named Orcus which could also have an influence. They first featured in the epic poem *Beowulf*, one of Tolkien's greatest influences. Tolkien's lecture essay, *Beowulf: the Monsters and the Critics*, is well worth checking out. It's Tolkien's version of the orc that has had the most lasting effect on the fantasy genre, so it's this type of orc we'll focus on.

- The perennial bad guy. Humanoid, grotesque and dirty, they usually make up the ranks of whatever evil force is at work. There is an element of fear behind why they serve.
- They tend to have sickly coloured skin, from greens and greys and even reds. Their appearance can be boar-like, with tusks and snouts.
- They have a ferocious attitude and are somewhat mindless. Portrayed as stupid, but that's misleading. They can craft weapons and treat injuries.
- The strongest orc tends to be the leader, though the position is often subject to challenges. A primitive way of social organisation.
- They love 'man flesh' and don't appear to put much effort into cooking it. They're known to eat each other too.
- They loathe humanity with a burning passion.
- Hang around with other brutish creatures, like wargs, trolls or toothy dogs.
- Tend to live in caves or hovels in tribe-like communes.
- Female orcs? Good question. In *Lord of the Rings* they're portrayed as being spawned from the earth.

Dwarves

- The modern fantasy idea likely stems from the dvergar of Norse mythology. They were said to have been as old as the gods themselves, living in the mountains and pounding their anvils.
- In high fantasy, the modern dwarf was first introduced in The Hobbit. Brave and fierce, they were artisans and

warriors, small and stout, rooted in tradition. And above all, they love a bit of coin and anything shiny or precious.

- They stand at a comfortable height to knee in the face.
- They can't get enough of mining and making weapons and armour.
- Usually ruled by a warrior-king.
- Female dwarves don't feature much. In *Lord of the Rings*, it was said dwarf women look like their men.
- Usually carry either an axe, swords, mattock (a weaponised version of a pickaxe), or a hammer.
- Tend to live in caves or cities built alongside or within mountains, or Viking-like communes with huts and longhouses, like in Feist's *Magician*.

Re-use: why deviate from the tried and tested?

I enjoy reading stories featuring elves and dwarves and orcs. I don't read many of them, though. I can imagine for those that do it can grow a bit tiresome, almost as if you're reading the same book over and over. "Oh look, the orcs have come to kill everyone."

In the original version of my short story *The General*, I had elves. It felt like I was cheating, that I wasn't really pushing myself to create. It's my story after all, why use someone else's idea? But I like elves. They're mysterious and good-natured and awesome with bows.

And that's the point. Despite the odd complaint, we still love these classic races. They're part of the reason we fell in love with fantasy. We enjoy the tropes that continue to enchant us. Dear old Gimli will forever hold a place in my heart. Deviating from the tried and tested can risk upsetting fans of these classic tropes.

Recycle: finding originality in a sea of lookalikes

It's tough being a writer these days. All the ideas, it seems, have been taken. But somewhere lays that vein of originality waiting to be mined and tapped into.

If you can, unshackle your mind and go wild with that plasticine trope in your mind. Morph it into all manner of shapes. Perhaps start with the classic trope and alter from there. Or start at the opposite end of the spectrum and work back from there until you find a level you like. Whatever you create is going to be different and unique because *you* created it.

This is what I decided to do for *The General*. I took the elf template and came up with the Vysi. They're smaller than humans, with eyes three times the size and giant ears the shape of a mouse's. I kept that elvish connection with nature I love so much, but even with those slight changes I found that readers appreciated the effort and difference. It gave them a new experience, something readers seek in stories.

Rubbish: starting from scratch

It's no easy feat coming up with an entirely new race of people. Especially when so many have been done. We've seen humanoid lizards and the Tsuranuanni in Feist's works. Adrian Tchaikovsky has a whole world full of unique races with affinities to different insects, such as beetles, wasps, mantids and spiders in his Shadows of the Apt series.

It's certainly possible to come up with your own. Unfortunately, I can't offer much help on that front; it's down to you, but as we've seen, there are ways to change things up. Expend some creative energy and see what you can make.

Cartography

It's time to don those geography caps; we're going back to high school. This chapter looks at the nature of things and how they're formed—oceans, seas, rivers, lakes, and deserts, forests, mountains, hills, swamps, snow, ice, and volcanoes—things you'll need to know and understand when it comes to making your own maps.

It's also important to remember that this is just a guide. A big part of fantasy is about creating new worlds. It's up to you whether to change the rules or not. This, at least, provides a starting point from which you can deviate.

Oceans and seas

Throughout history, humanity has made its home by the sea. Around half of the world's population live within coastal zones. It provides a multitude of opportunities to survive—food, water, bathing, energy sources, tactical advantages over enemies. It's unsurprising then, that many fantasy stories feature a sea of some kind. Here are a few things to consider.

- Oceans form over millions of years. Various theories exist as to how they came about. Some say the earth was struck by a water-rich meteoroid. The more likely theory is that they were formed by water vapour and other gases escaping from hydrothermal vents at the bottom of the ocean. You might have seen them on Blue Planet. Other sources are rivers and rain.

- Mankind needs oceans to survive. They produce over half of the oxygen in the atmosphere. Oceans absorb the heat of the sun, transfer it to the atmosphere and distribute it around the world by ocean currents, thereby regulating the weather.

- 'Ocean' and 'sea' are terms often used interchangeably, though there is a difference between them. Seas are smaller than oceans, usually located where the land and ocean meet. They are often partially enclosed by land. Raymond Feist's map of Midkemia from his *Riftwar Saga* is a good example of a fantasy map with various seas.

Rivers

Rivers are the veins of the planet, carrying fresh, life-giving water across the land. Many major civilizations have founded their homes along rivers, such as the Mesopotamians, the Egyptians and Chinese, and most great cities around the world are built upon rivers: London and the Thames, Rome and the Tiber, Dublin and the Liffey.

- Most rivers start life as a stream trickling down a mountain slope. These streams can come from underground springs, melting snow and ice or rainwater. The beginning of a river is known as a headwater.

- Rivers take their shape by following cracks and folds in the land. Small streams join together until they reach a size big enough to be classed as a river. No two rivers are the same. Each shapes the land in its own way.

- The land is shaped by the river as it makes its way to the ocean, eroding rock and carving out valleys. Rivers can change over time depending on the makeup of the river bed—soil, sand, rock, clay.

- Rivers widen and narrow and take snaking routes, called meanders.

- The small streams which flow into a river are known as tributaries.

- I'm sure you know what a river bank is. These areas are rich in nutrients as a result of flooding, but they also provide protection from flood damage, as well as filtering run-off from the land.

- The end of a river is known as a mouth or delta. Lands flatten and the current loses speed, usually around the point it meets the sea, lake or ocean.

- Some rivers flow year-round, others are seasonal and form during wet seasons.

- A river can be a kilometre long or stretch the length of a continent. Some examples of the lengths of real-life rivers: Nile – 6,853km long, Amazon – 6,992km, Mersey -112km (I'm from Liverpool, I had to include it), Congo – 4,700km.

- Some countries have no rivers—there are eighteen on earth—and others have shit loads. Russia, for example, has around 100,000.

- Many cities and towns and villages you find in fantasy stories are located close to rivers and streams. It makes sense, for it's the rivers that make those locations so ideal.

Lakes

There are a fair few lakes on earth. Around 117 million to be precise. They litter the land and invariably find their way into fantasy maps too.

- A lake is a body of water surrounded by land. They are found in every kind of environment: mountains, deserts, on plains, near coasts.
- They vary in size, from ponds to seas. The landlocked Caspian Sea is arguably the largest lake on earth.
- Lakes can form in various ways. Water can fill craters left by dormant or dead volcanoes, by glaciers, or from craters left by meteors or asteroids.
- Lakes evolve over time, and like humans, they age. Over hundreds and thousands of years, their basins fill with sediment and vegetation, growing shallower until eventually, they dry up.
- Most lakes are fed by rivers, streams, run-off from the land, and rain.

Deserts

The desert is a unique environment filled with a host of challenges. They feature quite often in fantasy books. The sand city of Dorne from *A Song of Ice and Fire* springs to mind. Here are a few things to keep in mind when including them:

- The standard definition of a desert is an area receiving less than 10 inches (or 250mm) of precipitation a year, i.e. rain, snow, sleet.
- Deserts are formed by the weather. Most people assume that deserts are sandy, arid places, but in fact, the largest desert on earth is Antarctica, which receives around 200mm of precipitation a year.
- Deserts are not static, rather they change over time through a process known as desertification. This involves the desert expanding its borders. As an example, 1,000 square miles of Chinese land turns to desert every year and in Africa a belt of forest known as 'The Great Green Wall' has been planted around deserts.
- Some deserts are flat, consisting of rock and sand. The Sahara is one example. Others contain rocky mountains, such as those in North America.
- Deserts tend to cover vast areas and contain little life and low vegetation cover.

Forests

Forests are home to a lot of fantasy settings. Fangorn Forest in *Lord of the Rings*. Elvandar in the *Riftwar Saga*. There is an air of mystery to them: the unusual sounds, the patches of darkness and light, countless places for secret watchers to hide. The forest breeds sanctuary, danger, curiosity and possibility, such that readers love them. Here are the guiding principles to do with how they form and the effect they have on the wider world.

- Forests can grow anywhere in which the temperature rises above 10 degrees Celsius during the warmest months and sees average rainfall (or precipitation in general) of more than 8 inches a year.

- The difference between a wood and a forest lies in the extent of the canopy. A forest has canopies covering over 10% of the sky. A wood's is between 5 and 10%.

- The type of trees which grow in a forest is dependent upon the temperature, amount of rainfall, and soil. For example in cool, subpolar regions, hardy conifers like pines, spruces and larches, dominate the land. This type of forest is known as a taiga or boreal forest. They have long winters, with between 10 and 20 inches of rainfall a year.

- In forests of a warmer climate, the type of trees mix between conifers and broad-leaved deciduous trees (those which lose their leaves each year). The substrate here is mostly brown soil with sandy sections.

- Deciduous forests occur where the average temperature is above 10 degrees Celsius for at least six months of the year with precipitation above 16 inches. The types of trees found in these forests include elms, oaks, birches, maples, beeches, and aspens. The ground here is a brown soil, rich in nutrients.

- Tropical rainforests develop in more humid conditions. Heavy rainfall, about 100 inches per year, supports evergreens which possess broad leaves to capture light. The soil is rich in iron or aluminium which gives it a red or yellow hue.

Mountains and volcanoes

Mountains make for a challenging and unpredictable setting, with difficult pathways, howling winds and freezing temperatures. Think of all of the scenes featuring mountains where someone is thrown into oblivion below, grasping at the air as they plummet.

The Vale in *A Song of Ice and Fire* is kingdom surround by a mountain range, with the main keep in The Eyrie built on a mountain. Gandalf tried to lead the Fellowship over Moria, only to turn back. They provide obstacles to get around, challenges to overcome. And they make a great lair for bad guys. Here are a few things to keep in mind:

- Mountains are the foundations of life. They act as water towers, manipulating the weather to create rain and snow which in turn forms streams, which turn into rivers. Without them, there would be no drinking water and no habitats in which life could survive.

- There is no generally accepted definition for how tall a mountain has to be. Some say 1,000 feet, others 2,000. A chap named Roderick Peattie came up with a subjective definition which I'm quite a fan of. He said a mountain ought to be defined based on its ability to command attention, their impact on human imagination, and their individuality.

- Certain types of mountains can grow. Tectonic plate movement pushes the Earth's crust upwards. Everest, for instance, grows around 4mm a year.

- Sticking with the types of a mountain, there are four in all: fold, block, dome, and volcanic. Most are found in groups, referred to as, you guessed it, ranges. The highest point is known as a peak or summit, the bottom the base.

- **Block mountains.** These form when a slab of land breaks off at a fault line in the crust and is forced up as two tectonic plates push together.
- **Dome mountains.** These occur when magma within the earth forces the ground upward, like a nasty boil. The magma doesn't break the surface.
- **Fold mountains.** These are the most common type of mountain and occur when two tectonic plates push against each other over many years, making more folds.
- **Volcanoes.** These are vital to earth's survival, providing chemical elements and minerals to water, the land and atmosphere. There are four types with differing appearances: shield (large with gentle slopes), stratovolcano (large with steep slopes), caldera (shaped like a cauldron), and cinder cone (a straight, steep mound). All but the cinder cone volcano tend to have more than one vent through which magma erupts. On Earth, more volcanoes exist beneath the ocean.
- Plateaus are creations of mountains. Blocks of earth drop and lie next to each other to produce flat land. The Tibetan plateau is one example.
- The length of mountain ranges can vary. The mid-ocean ridge, for example, is about 40,389 miles long.

Hills and valleys

In the vast plains in between our cities, mountains, rivers and other landmarks, there lie other features which bring life and richness to our worlds: hills and valleys. Throughout history, these points in the land have made for terrific tactical and defensive positions. Rome, for instance, was built on seven hills so invaders could be sighted from afar.

- A **hill** is a piece of land with sloping sides which rises higher than everything around it. They're usually less steep than a mountain. The top is called the summit.
- Hills can form in a variety of ways. One natural way is the result of a geological process known as faulting—the Earth's crust shifts and moves and changes the landscape, forming hills. They can also form as a result of glacial activity.
- Hills are also formed by erosion—bits of rock, soil, and sediment get washed away to form a pile. But just as erosion can create hills, it can destroy them too.
- Hills can be made by people. They go by the name of mounds.
- There are different types of hills: A **drumlin** is a long hill formed by the movement of glaciers. A **butte** is a steep-sided, flat-topped hill which stands alone in a flat area. A **puy** is a conical, volcanic hill.
- A **valley** is a depressed area of land, usually shaped like a 'U' or 'V', formed by the forces of gravity, water, or ice. Rivers and streams cut through valleys and are usually responsible for the 'V' shape. Glaciers form valleys by slowly creeping downhill, picking up rocks on their way and grinding up anything in its path. These usually leave a 'U' shape. There's another type of valley called a rift; giant, gaping formations where two pieces of the Earth's crust have been separated. The Great Rift Valley is one example.

Wetlands

Swamps, bogs, mires, and marshes can provide for an interesting feature on a map. The Dead Marshes from *Lord of the Rings* is one example which pops to mind. In my experience, they're pretty underused. Here's a bit about them:

- Wetland is the all-encompassing term for swamps, marshes, bogs, and so on. Wetlands are any bit of land saturated by water. That is where the water level is at, near or above the surface of the ground.
- Wetlands perform crucial functions, such as flood control and coastal storm buffers.
- Swamps are a common type of wetland: areas of land permanently saturated or filled with water, some even covered by it. They come in two types: freshwater swamps, which are found inland, and saltwater swamps which are found, unsurprisingly, by coastal areas.
- **Freshwater swamps**: these form around lakes and streams. Cypress and tupelo trees are found in such places, along with Spanish moss which hangs from trees, and duckweed which covers the water's surface. An example of a freshwater swamp would be the Everglades.
- **Saltwater swamps**: form along tropical coastlines. Seawater pools during high tides over time. Usually, mangrove trees are found in these places.

Snow and ice

The snowy realm beyond the Wall in *A Song of Ice and Fire* is a mysteriously appealing place, filled with giants, White

Walkers, and dire wolves. It's an iconic setting in the books and TV series. But how did it all come about? How did it get so cold? And how did all that ice form? In looking at the history of Antarctica we can gain an understanding of the nature of these icy planes and how they occur:

- It's not exactly certain how Antarctica was formed. Very helpful, I know. At one time, it was a land not dissimilar to the European Alps, with alpine mountains and all kinds of flora and fauna thriving there. Until it all turned a bit cold. The average depth of the ice covering the continent is about a mile thick. That's one hell of a change.

- One leading theory is that a reduction in Earth's carbon dioxide levels—thereby cooling the global temperatures—as well as changes in its orbit, caused a great degree of cooling. It led to glaciers forming on the land, which grew over millions of years.

The Trusty Steed

"*Arise, arise, Riders of Theoden! Fell deeds awake, fire and slaughter! Spears shall be shaken, shields shall be splintered. A sword day, a red day, ere the sun rises! Ride now, ride now! Ride for ruin and the world's ending!*"

King Theoden, *The Return of the King*

Horses play iconic roles in the fantasy genre, fearlessly carrying heroes into battle, facing down dragons (and being eaten by them), and taking characters across countries and continents. But there's much more to a horse than a means of transportation and great care ought to be adopted when featuring them in a tale, lest you draw the wrath of the horse gods. Below you'll find a few things to keep in mind.

Make no assumptions

For some of us, interactions with horses are few and far between. We may occasionally drive by one in a field at 50mph, or see one grazing during a foray into the countryside. We probably see horses more on TV than we do in reality. It, therefore, makes sense that we wouldn't know too much about them: how they behave and such. Herein lies one of the biggest complaints from readers I've encountered: the lack of understanding.

To fill the void of this lack of experience, it's important to learn. Assume you know nothing at all and start with the basics. After a few minutes of research you'll know that a female horse is called a mare, a male a stallion, a young female a filly, a young male a colt. The average horse can gallop around 27 miles per hour. They have 360-degree vision and bigger eyes than any other land-based mammal. The height of horses is, in some countries, measured in a unit called 'hands' (approx. 4 inches), something you may have encountered while reading fantasy.

Let's bring George R.R. Martin into the equation here. He studies medieval life so has an understanding of the horses of those times and uses this knowledge to tremendous effect in his stories. Here's a bit of that knowledge for your benefit.

Horses had three main purposes in the Middle Ages—war, agriculture and transport—and they were bred with these purposes in mind. Here are a few different breeds, some of which feature in *A Song of Ice and Fire:*

> *Destrier* - This was a horse renowned for its capabilities in war, though it was pretty uncommon due to their high cost— only knights and other aristocrats could afford them. Well-trained, strong, fast and agile, they were described as "tall and majestic and with great strength". The average height of a destrier in the Middle Ages was 12 to 14 hands (48 to 56 inches).

> *Palfrey* - Equal to a destrier in price and popular with nobles and high ranking knights for riding, hunting and ceremonies. The smooth gait of palfreys made riding

comfortable, so they were the preferred choice when travelling long distances.

Courser/charger – Preferred for fierce, hectic battles. Fast and strong. Not as expensive as the destrier, though still valuable. The most common of all warhorses.

Rounsey/rouncey – General purpose horses. The 'ordinary' one. Cheap and readily available. Ideal for both riding and war. Used by squires, men at arms, and poorer knights.

Jennet – A horse smaller than a rounsey, known for their quiet nature. Used mostly for riding because of their smooth, ambling gait, though at times adopted as cavalry.

Hobby – How could I leave out an Irish horse? My family would disown me. Hobbies were well-regarded for their swiftness, effective in skirmishes, though used infrequently in combat.

If ever you're unsure of something or want to know more, why not try riding yourself? It's the best lesson you can get. Feeling the chafe of the saddle and the strain on your muscles, whiffing the scent of the horse, and hearing the sounds as it trots along a muddy trail. I'm sure there's a riding school not far away from you. Or you could reach out to the writing community. There's been many a time when fellow writers have offered their knowledge and experience on particular subjects to me, and you'll be surprised how many people have experience of horse riding.

Treat your horses like characters

Your horse lives and breathes, just like your characters. It tires, grows hungry, thirsty, can get injured—limitations all living creatures possess. Disregarding them risks damaging the credibility of your tale.

Horses feature heavily in George R.R. Martin's *Tales of Dunk and Egg*. The hedge knight Dunk has a close bond with his mounts, for as a knight, he relies on them. He makes sure his squire, Egg, feeds and waters them every day, and after a long ride, brushed and washed down. When one sadly dies, he buries it and later recalls memories of it.

As with any of your pets, horses require caring for, and a neglected horse is one that will suffer injuries, grow fatigued, and die.

There are other benefits to fleshing out your four-legged means of getting from A to B. A character building a relationship with a horse, or any pet for that matter is a great source of empathy. Characters considerate towards others tend to be likeable. Take Blondie from *The Good, the Bad, and the Ugly*. He's a killer, but we're drawn to him because, other than being cool as fuck amongst other things, he respects and cares for his horse.

It's a possible source of conflict too. If a horse your reader has grown attached to is at risk of harm, or heaven forbid is harmed (you cruel bastard), the reader feels it too. Just look at *Black Beauty*.

If you're new to riding, you're going to fall

Riding a horse is a skill which requires a lot of practice. *A lot* of practice. Not only does the horse have to be well trained to handle a rider, but the rider must also understand how to ride the horse. A character with no experience or knowledge of riding would be unable to jump on a horse and ride away to safety. Convenient yes, realistic no.

You don't have to go through the ins and outs of learning how to ride a horse in your story. That'd be boring. Just acknowledge your character is training and improving. A few things they would learn for instance would be lightly squeezing the horse's sides with their legs to get it to walk, or squeezing again to set it into a trot. Or to make the horse stop, lean back and pull on the reins.

While falling off a horse can potentially lead to serious injury—another source of conflict—it also makes for great entertainment. Who doesn't enjoy a bit of schadenfreude?

Each horse has its own personality

All animals tend to have their own personality: belligerent, curious, nervous, friendly. Featuring this in your stories not only gives it more life, but it also presents an opportunity for you to build connections between your characters and their steeds. You may have a character who simply does not get along with their horse, which nips at him, rears up, kicks out, and runs off. Or you may be like Aragorn who whispers sweet nothings in their ears and bends them to his will.

A few helpful horse adjectives

The world of horses is a detailed one, and taking advantage of those details will, as George R.R. Martin has proven, make your stories even more immersive. Here are a few words to describe the colourations and breeds of your fantasy mounts:

> *Bay:* a horse ranging in colour from light reddish brown to dark brown with black points, these points being the mane, tail and lower legs.

> *Chestnut:* similar colour to the bay, though lacking any black points.

> *Buckskin:* a lighter colour of the bay horse, though maintaining the black points.

> *Pinto:* multi-coloured with patches of brown, white and/or black. The black and white variation is known as a *piebald*, a breed which features in *A Song of Ice and Fire* — .Pod's old piebald rounsey.

So that's the basics of horses and fiction covered. It may sound silly, but they have the potential to make or break a story for some readers. The Ride of the Rohirrim in the Return of the King still brings a tear to my eye. It's such a powerful scene, and the horses played a role in that.

Ride for ruin, and the world's ending.

Making Monsters

The fantasy genre is rich with imagined monsters, creatures, and beasts. Creations which haunt our dreams and give us paranoid thoughts when we hear that inexplicable bump in the middle of the night.

In this chapter, we'll take a look at some of the more common monsters found in fantasy before turning to look at some of the ways you can find inspiration for your own.

Types of monsters

The same types of monsters crop up in fantasy and most of them have consistent traits. Below, we'll look at some of them, but there's nothing to stop you from deviating. In doing so you may find that original angle.

Demons

Demons are probably one of the most common types of monster I come across in fantasy. They feature in James Barclay's *Noonshade*, quite heavily in Raymond Feist's *Riftwar Saga*. H.P. Lovecraft had his famous demon, Cthulhu, and Tolkien had the Balrog. But what is a demon exactly? Let's have a look at some of the most common tropes:

- They are inherently evil, possessing an unwavering desire to break into our realm from whatever plane they come from and wreak havoc on life as we know it.
- In terms of appearance, the classic demon is somewhat goat-like, with horns like a ram, cloven hooves, red skin. Some have wings and their size can vary from mountainous to minuscule.
- Contemporary demons sometimes take human form, ranging from grotesque old men to beautiful, seductive women—you won't believe how many pictures of sexy demons there are on the internet.
- In most instances, they're summoned by some beardy lunatic and the good guys have to somehow banish it to whence it came.

Trolls

Trolls have been around a while. My earliest recollection of a troll was in the kid's story *Three Billy Goats Gruff*. The troll in that tale was depicted as a grotesque brute that ate anybody foolish enough to cross the bridge he lived under. I avoided bridges for years. One of my favourite scenes in the *Lord of the Rings* series is when the cave troll bursts through the doors in Moria and bellows a roar.

But trolls come in different shapes and sizes. The Moomins were trolls and hardly the kind to rip your arms from your body.

Here are a few common tropes:

- The word 'troll' is an old Norse word which means fiend, demon or giant. You can kind of see where they get their reputation from.

- Trolls are diverse, ranging from massive, bloodthirsty monsters to cute and friendly gnomes.
- The big ones like to smash things with tree trunks or giant weapons forged to wreak havoc.
- Can withstand a boatload of arrows, unless you shoot it in the head while standing on its shoulders.
- Tend to be pretty dim with vulnerabilities to certain things. For example, in *The Hobbit*, the three trolls turned to stone when touched by daylight. In other depictions, trolls are vulnerable to fire. However, other versions portray them as crafty, cunning creatures.
- They tend to live in isolation, either in forests or caves.

Ents

I know ents don't feature broadly across the fantasy genre, but I bloody love them. The last march of the ents in *The Two Towers* still gives me the chills.

But I include ents to illustrate how you can make a monster out of literally anything. There's something terrifying about a change in the behaviour of the familiar. A tree that can crush people? Harmless to armless.

And it shows that you can create nice monsters and not evil ones. The ents are maybe one of the most likeable creatures in the entire fantasy genre, and I'd say that's because of the rich history Tolkien gave them. We gain an understanding of their character and perspective from the likes of the way they talk, how they conduct their affairs, how they lament the loss of their ent wives. It's a wonderful example of the lengths you can go to when crafting your monsters.

Forging fell beasts

What should we consider when making a monster? Let's take a look at some tips offered by bestselling horror writer, Philip Athans:

- It should be different and scary; something we've never seen before;

- Dangerous, threatening, and violent. Think of those scenes of pure carnage that make you realise how much blood is in a human body. Or bodies with grotesque and inexplicable injuries. Think of your most sensitive parts of the body and torment them with your pen. A lot of people are scared of injuring their eyes.

- The monster disrupts the predator/prey relationship. No longer are humans at the top of the food chain.

- It should be unpredictable. Humans can sometimes gauge what can happen next. Try to make that as difficult as possible. The less your characters know about what a monster can and can't do, the better. It's this unpredictability that will keep your readers on the edge of their seats, playing into the power of the imagination.

- Perspective. Is your monster a creation of pure evil, hell bent on destruction? Is it a force for good, striving to save others? Is it misunderstood, wanting to fit in, to be like humans? Is it conflicted in some way? Playing with the perspectives of your monsters can give you that unique edge. A cave troll afraid of fighting? *Grendel* by John Gardner is a good example of this.

Monsters from mythology

If the ideas still aren't flowing, try turning to mythology. This was a massive influence for Tolkien. We see the influences in the Balrog, the Watcher in the Water outside Moria, Shelob and of course, cave trolls. Sauron too has something demonic about him.

Norse mythology is rich with monsters. The giants, also known as the 'devourers', are spirits of death and darkness. A number of devourers took the form of creatures. There's Fenrir the giant wolf who slew the god Odin. Nidhogg the serpent that gnaws at the roots of the world-tree. Sleipnir, Odin's eight-legged horse, and Jormungand, a sea serpent which surrounds the land of humanity.

Greek mythology is a whole new level of monsters, from the minotaur, Cyclops, and Medusa, to Scylla— a multi-headed sea serpent—and the three-headed dog and guardian of the underworld, Cerberus.

In exploring these myths it gives you a basis to create your own monster. You can experiment with features or traits, piece together the anatomy of your beast, and adapt them to your world and setting.

The fear factor

Another method you can adopt is to study what people fear. Think of all the phobias people have of creatures. Fear of spiders is a common one. Some people loathe how they look with their swift-moving legs and bristly bodies and fangs. It's these little details that make people's skin crawl. As an exercise, think of something you're afraid of and note the details A good thing to do is jot down a few of the things that creep you out the most. Combine them with features of other beastly creatures you dislike and see what you get.

In a short story I'm working on at the moment I wanted to include some type of arachnid but was conscious of going for the obvious. I played around with the features, thinking of how it moved and the sounds those movements could make. I morphed the image of a spider into something more centipedal with a cavernous, circular mouth filled with rows of serrated teeth. You never know, in conjuring something terrifying you may overcome your fears.

Don't just stop at your own fears. What are other people afraid of? Google phobias. Here are the top five phobias of all time, according to this article anyway:

- Cynophobia – the fear of dogs;
- Agoraphobia – the fear of open spaces;
- Acrophobia – the fear of heights;
- Ophidiophobia – the fear of snakes
- Arachnophobia – the fear of spiders.

If you can make a monster using a fear of heights I commend you. Maybe some kind of creature that propels you into the air?

Using allegories

One thing to help come up with ideas for your monster is allegories—what does this monster represent or mean, either morally or politically. For instance, Bram Stoker's *Dracula* is said to represent a fear of foreigners and disease which existed at the time of its publication. It's a more technical approach but one that can work very well.

Fantasy and Religion

Religion and belief systems feature a great deal in the fantasy genre, and it's unsurprising why. Religion, faiths and beliefs shape our lives in a multitude of ways, providing purpose, meaning and structure. That's not to say everyone's lives, but a good number.

It's a very broad topic which I've tried to condense into this sole chapter. It first looks at how religion can shape fantasy worlds, how it can affect characters, how you can create your own religions, and finishes with the opinions of readers.

Before we march on, I wish to make it clear that this is just an examination of religion within the fantasy genre. Everybody is free to hold their own beliefs and the last thing I wish is to cause any offence. I was raised a Roman Catholic, went to church every week until the age of fifteen, even served as an altar boy. I'm a non-believer now, but that doesn't mean I look at religion with scorn like so many do. My aim here is to be as objective as possible.

Defining religion

Religion can be construed in different ways; it doesn't help there are three different dictionary definitions:

- The belief and worship of an 'all-powerful' figure, such as a god or goddess (monotheism). There can be more than one central figure too (polytheism).
- A system of faith and worship.
- A pursuit or interest followed with devotion.

When we think of our own religions, one thing which features heavily is *faith*. It's faith in a belief or religion which makes it real in minds and hearts. What gives us faith? Teachings which we agree with? Answers to questions we seek the answers to? Miracles, religious texts, prayers, masses and sermons which imbue us with purpose? I don't think there's any catch-all answer.

To me, religion is a good thing. At the core of all religions are teachings which tell us how to treat others, guidelines to help give some structure to this chaotic world of ours. It's a vehicle for good, but sometimes vehicles get hijacked.

How religion can shape fantasy worlds

Let's begin by looking at our own world. We've seen the Crusades and more recently the rise and fall of Islamic State. Religion has been used as the justification for these conquests, which saw hundreds of thousands die and more displaced. Borders changed, cities levelled and new ones built, groups of people snuffed from history. I'm straying more into the implications of conquest generally here, but it shows the influential reach a belief can have.

On a less violent level, how can religion shape societies? Canon law and the beliefs of the church in Medieval England dictated the lives of many, women in particular. For instance, canon law defined a woman as 'a sort of infant' and gave husbands permission to beat their wives if he thought them lazy or disobedient.

What of religion and your secondary world? What do your people have faith in? What do they believe, if anything at all? How has time before your story shaped your world? What role, if any, did religion play? Things like weddings, funerals, baptisms are all religious customs. How does the religion of your world impact these aspects of your characters' lives?

More questions have to be asked if magic exists in your world. What's the relationship between that magic and religion? Are they separate or interlinked? Do they conflict with each other? How do different characters view religion and how does magic influence religion?

A pretty common feature of fantasy religions is that they tend to be *true*. Gods and goddesses do exist, manifesting themselves in different ways, such as forces or energies or demi-gods, as well as ancient prophecies which come to pass. If religion is true, what role does faith play? Is it less important?

It's the discussions of gods and goddesses which help create what they are. Look at Bram Stoker's *Dracula*. Dracula hardly features in the story, yet we learn much about him as it progresses. In keeping the distance between humanity and gods and goddesses you help to create that mysterious, all-powerful air.

How can religion affect characters?

A great way to explore religion in a fantasy world is to have a character, or several, who hold conflicting beliefs. At one end of the belief spectrum are fundamentalists. At the other, sceptics, atheists, people who believe some parts but not all. Some of these groups actively oppose each other, such as zealots and atheists.

Just as we have the believers, we also have the manipulators. People who take advantage of religion and people's need to find purpose, answers, structure, and warping their minds for their own gain. Looking into real-world cults is a great way to get to the heart of this. It's important to keep in mind that an antagonist inspired by what we would deem an evil religion ought to believe wholeheartedly that they are right and justified in their actions; they must think they're the good guy. It's what God wants after all.

It's important to be mindful of how you portray religious characters. Quite a common occurrence is the religious 'knuckleheads'. Brandon Sanderson discusses this with reference to writer Dan Brown. Sanderson argues that Brown views religious characters as fools who should be proven wrong. Sanderson recommends avoiding this trope. He finds it reductionist and offensive, and he's not alone.

Another aspect of religion which creates conflict is contradictions. People interpret religious texts in different ways. Christianity, for instance, has numerous branches, the Westboro Baptist Church just one extreme example. It's important to remember that as a writer if you introduce contradictions, you're creating conflict which in turn creates a plot point.

Readers can expect something to develop out of it, so if you go to the trouble, be sure it's going somewhere.

Religion can provide context for character's actions too. They can take messages from forces which shape how they live. How does religion help characters interpret your world? This is a point we'll come to in more detail below.

Think about the religious roles your characters could play? Are there shamans, priests or priestesses, a Pope-like figure? Just look at how influential the High Sparrow became in *Game of Thrones*.

Playing creator

If you're to feature religion in detail in your stories, it's likely going to impact many strata of your society and therefore, it should be a big factor when world-building. The swell folks over at Fantasy Faction published an excellent article on this very topic, and in it suggested a few questions to ask yourself when thinking about your own religion:

"1) **Where did we come from?** Your religion should have some explanation for how the world came to be. You might say, "well, science explains that." That's fine, but we're talking religion here. Look at the world around us. There's a constant tug of war between religion and science. Perhaps science does explain everything in your world, but unless science is also the religion of the day (which is fine, by the way), you need to have some explanation for creation in your religion.

2) **What happens when we die?** You have to answer questions about the afterlife with your new religion. Heaven, Hades, Valhalla, Nirvana, Maya, whatever it is, you need to have some explanation, tradition, story, or theory within your religion about what happens when people die.

3) **How should we act while we're here?** Your religion should provide some kind of moral code. What that moral code says is pretty much wide open, but most religions provide some kind of list, law, code, ethics, what have you for its followers. Within this moral code will be some aspect of discipline as well, which will probably tie into what happens when someone dies."

These are just a handful of key questions to ask yourself. Writer Orson Scott Card provides a great list too which you can read by clicking here, or head to https://www.writing-world.com/sf/card.shtml.

What I'd add to this list is: **what do we regard as important in life?** When a lot of religions and beliefs were first formed, the things which people revered most in their lives were in the skies, i.e. the sun and stars. The sun, in particular, was seen as the giver of life, the conqueror of darkness. It can be argued that the heart of every religion boils down to the struggle between good and evil, light and darkness, and the essence of that battle stems from day and night, how the sun falls each day, giving way to evil darkness, only then to rise again and save humanity. Astronomy played a significant role in people's lives too. It was used for navigation, gauging the passage of time, and as a guide for when to plant crops. These were all important things in people's lives and as such, they became the focus.

For religions to spread and catch on, you need to think logistics. The rise of Catholicism, for example, was partly down to preachers prepared to travel countless miles. My Great-Uncle Paddy was a Catholic missionary in Sierra Leone who tried to establish a church there. Every time he built one it was torn down by other religious groups. Again, another example of conflict.

The opinions of readers

I found an insightful thread on r/fantasy to do with religion, packed with a wide range of opinions, some of which I thought would be quite helpful. Here are just a few. You can read the full thread by clicking here.

> **rake_the_great:** I'm not against people who are religious being evil - it definitely happens in the real world - but it bugs me when the author uses it because they don't have the motivation to come up with something interesting on their own. It was annoying when Dan Brown and Assassin's Creed did it, and so when this formula comes up again, it feels degrading to something that's very important to me personally.

> **Petros-Tr** - Fantasy books with Gods that actually make an appearance (not just mentioned) are my favourite. Powder Mage, Lightbringer, The Chronicle of the Exile etc.

Theloftytransient - If an author doesn't think about religion intelligently or has studied it from an anthropology perspective, it's pretty obvious and painful. Hate the "Christianity applies to everything even fantasy" trope. I also don't like the "all religions are cults or evil" and "atheists are the wisest" trope.

Archprimus - I don't like being overwhelmed with religion in books in all honesty. When I was reading Mistborn I remember Sazed used to take a few pages to inform Vin of different religions in the past. And I liked it too, learning about it because it was fun.

Enasor - While I do not usually mind the inclusion of religion within works of fantasy, I would like to see more books where it isn't such a prominent theme.

Schmii - I love religion in fantasy especially if an author can create a religion that feels rather complex. I just think religion is so interesting because it can bring people together and tear people apart.

Religion is a complicated topic. We've just scratched the surface on these few pages. If you want religion, beliefs and faiths to form a prominent part of your fantasy story then it's going to take a bit of time and effort. Hopefully, the tips in this chapter will set you on the right path.

Finding Inspiration:
The Middle Ages

I. Archery

Archery features heavily in fantasy; it's one of the reasons why I love the genre so much. But I've learned—the hard way (always the hard way isn't it?)—that doing your research when it comes to things such as this is necessary. Not only will you look like a genius for knowing crazy shit about bows, but you'll have a tale enriched with pleasing detail.

I've done a bit of that research for you, and below you'll find a nifty guide to all things archery.

The arrow

The nock is to hold the arrow to the bowstring. The feathery part next to the nock is known as the fletching, and the bit below that is known as the cresting.

The body of the arrow is known as the shaft. Depending on the type of arrow, the end of the shaft was either sharpened into a point or fitted with an arrowhead. Early arrowheads were made from bone, stone or horn, with metal arrowheads like bronze and iron, developed later.

There were various ways of affixing the head to the shaft (I can hear your dirty minds working). An early method was using a glue-type resin made from plants. Another was a process known as hafting, which involved softening the shaft with heat or water so that slits could be cut into it. The arrowhead, carved in a suitable way, was then fitted into the slits. Another process was split-shafting. This involved splitting the end of the shaft lengthwise, inserting the arrowhead in the gap, and securing it using sinew or rope.

Things were less technical methods too. Some lazy bastards just spat on the end of the shaft and shoved the arrowhead on before they fired, enough for the head to stay on the shaft and lodge in the body of an enemy.

The feathers used in medieval fletching came from goose, turkey, duck, grouse, pheasant, even pigeons. Goose, however, was deemed the best. This type of feather possesses oils which make it waterproof, to a certain extent. The size of the feather depended on the purpose of the arrow.

Arrows decelerate quickly once fired, and the velocity of an arrow, as well as the type of bow by which it was fired, was important in penetrating metal armour. Here's a brief distance/damage guide to give you an idea:

- From 80 metres (approx. 240 feet) an arrow would merely dent steel armour, and leave a knight feeling pretty invincible.

- From around 30 metres away an arrow would puncture steel but would cause only a bruise, the padding beneath the armour coming to the rescue.
- From 20 metres away an arrow would penetrate clean and deep, as the French and Genoese crossbowmen discovered at the Battle of Crécy (1346)—a battle won by the longbow, and one worth reading about.

Arrows were stored in quivers made from oiled canvas to keep them dry.

If shot by an arrow the only way to cleanly remove it was to push it through the wound and out the other side. If bone stood in the way, then depending on how good your doctor was, it was pulled free with forceps.

The bow

The short bow emerged first, but, as the name suggests, it had limited range, and as a result, limited effectiveness in battle. The longbow changed archery and warfare forever.

Most longbows were made from a curved stave of, amongst other woods, yew, ash, hazel, maple, and elm. Yew was deemed the best because it can withstand a great deal of tension. The strings tended to be made from hemp because it's strong, easy to manufacture and inelastic.

The longbow was somewhere between five and six feet tall and tended to match the height of the wielder to allow for a full draw. Like arrows, a bow was kept in an oiled canvas bag to keep it dry.

The shape of the bow was very important. There were a few different shapes, the main being:

- The **recurve**: a bow in which the tips curve away from the wielder. As the bow is drawn these curves straighten, and when loosed, snap back to propel the arrow at a greater velocity. To achieve the shape the tips were boiled in water.
- **Self-bow**: a simple bow made from a single piece of wood with the tips pointing away from the wielder.

How bows were used

Mastery of the bow required a great deal of practice. Training involved lining up and aiming at markers set at various distances and gradients. A key skill required of the archer was the ability to read the landscape to note any dips, rises or obstructions. The objective was to create a killing zone, rather than aiming for specific targets.

The act of notching the arrow to the bowstring is known as 'nocking', and with this, speed was everything—definitely not like me, fiddling for minutes just to get the arrow on the string, all the while swearing profusely. The arrow is then 'drawn' back, the string tightened. To keep it taut an archer had to be physically strong, with power generated from the muscles of the back. 'Loose' was the order to fire. "Nock, draw, loose."

So speed was important, and to accelerate the process in battle, arrows were stabbed into the ground before the archer.

Archers had to be mobile too. If shit hit the fan they had to move and adapt. Heavy armour was spared, with the emphasis on lightness and portability. If archers did get caught up in close combat most were armed with a blade of some kind, a popular one being a falchion—a one-handed, single-edged sword, similar to a machete, but with a cross guard.

Mounted archers became popular during the Iron Age, with the earliest depictions coming from the Parthians of Iran. If you thought shooting an arrow while standing still was tricky, how about loosing one from a charging horse?

Mounted archers provided a massive tactical advantage, able to harass the flanks of foes, cause disruption and confusion, and inflict casualties. The Parthian shot, as it was known, was a tactic which involved retreating from an enemy while turning the upper body and shooting backwards. Mounted archers were, however, pretty weak against a large force of foot archers, who had a much swifter rate of fire, as well as a bigger target to aim for.

The crossbow

I've opted to keep the crossbow separate from other types of bow due to the differences in its use and operation. Compared to the traditional bow, the crossbow was cumbersome. It was, however, easier to shoot and packed a hell of a punch. From close range, armour may well have been made of lard.

Some medieval crossbows were crafted with horn and sinew, as well as wood. Horn can take great strain, and sinew, such as that of the neck tendon of an ox, becomes stringy when hammered.

The biggest downside to the crossbow was the length of time it took to reload. With some of the earliest crossbows, the user had to sit down and pull the string back to load the bolt. A totally ideal method for warfare...

Devices were crafted to increase the reload speed. A rack and pinion—a winch-type contraption—was one such device. Another was a belt attachment which pulled the string back. Larger crossbows possessed another type of mechanism known as a windlass.

The crossbow was a weapon rarely used by the common folk. They were high-tech devices in their time, like the floppy disk in the nineties, and as a result, cost a pretty penny. But the good thing about them was that they were easy to use, and that meant pretty much anybody could learn how to wield one.

In warfare crossbowmen sometimes hid behind a large shield known as a pavise. One man held up the shield, while the crossbowmen worked away behind, firing, ducking, reloading. This tactic was also adopted with other types of bows.

As well as shields, crossbowmen, and archers too, tended to be protected by pike or billmen who formed defensive positions around them, known as hedgehogs, a tactic used to counter cavalry attacks.

So that's the basics of archery. To get more of a feel for it I highly recommend reading up on some famous battles in which bow and arrows played a decisive role. Crecy is perhaps one of the most famous. And why not try a bit of archery yourself? You'll be surprised how many archery ranges there are. Go out and feel what it's like to pull back a bowstring, feel the weight of the bow in your hands, the satisfaction of striking a target. It'll make the writing easier.

244 | A Fantasy Writers' Handbook

II. Armour

We march on from archery to armour. We all love a character with a unique set of armour: the baresark Rek from David Gemmell's *Legend* with his enchanted armour of bronze, or Tomas from Raymond Feist's *Riftwar Cycle* with his gleaming white armour that gifts him incredible power. Although these wonderful suits of armour exist in fantasy worlds, it's important to understand how armour works in the real world, even at a basic level. This guide will hopefully equip you with what you need to enrich your tales.

Medieval armour

The development of medieval armour kicked off during the Hundred Years War between the English and the French. English archers were butchering the French with arrow storms, wiping out their cavalry in particular. The French had to do something, and so an arms race ensued. Weapons were built to defeat armour, and armour built to withstand weapons. A vicious cycle with vicious motives.

Let's have a look at a few types of armour.

Chainmail

Mail was one of the first types of metal armour developed, arguably by the Celts, though other sources say its origins lie in Eastern Europe. A coat of mail was a complex web of metal rings interlocked with an iron rivet. Such coats were made from brass or iron, though steel was deemed best due to its toughness.

A jacket or coat of mail was usually worn with a hood, or coif, of the same material to protect the head and neck. As time marched on, small plates of leather or iron were added to the mail to protect key areas, such as the vital organs. These small plates were also known as scales.

Mail was particularly effective against glancing blows. In battle, you are trying to strike a moving target, so mail was sufficient as most blows were glancing ones. Clean, powerful strikes were needed to disable a foe wearing mail. Blunt weapons were effective, causing haemorrhaging and concussion. To combat that threat, padded garments, known as a doublet or gambeson, were worn underneath mail to provide added protection.

Mail was lightweight and flexible. Good for the mobile warrior. With all the links and chains it was laborious to make, but not difficult and was easily repaired. Another benefit to chain mail, a point which can slip the mind of writers, is that it was cheap and efficient, able to accommodate different sized warriors, unlike expensive plated armour, to which we now turn.

Plated armour

When we think of knights the image of rigid tin men that can withstand all manner of blows comes to mind. A knight's armour was made up of a lot of different pieces. Here's a breakdown of the key components:

Helmet – I'm sure you know this – armour for the head.

Visor – a plate that contained slits or holes for ventilation that could pivot up and down or open outwards over the wearer's face. Used to provide protection to the face.

Gorget – protection for the collar.

Pauldron – a vest-like piece providing protection over the upper back, breast and shoulders.

Breastplate – a plate that covers the upper chest area.

Fauld – an attachment to the breastplate that protected the abdomen.

Rerebrace – armour for the upper arm.

Vambrace – armour for the forearm. Also known as bracers.

Gauntlet – an armoured glove.

Cuisse – armour for the thigh.

Greave – a piece covering the lower leg.

Sabaton – foot armour, and sometimes a weapon. The toes could be fashioned into dagger-like points, useful when trying to break a shield wall.

It took a while to get ready, with the help of somebody else needed, usually squires, who began with the feet and worked up from there. Both doublets and chain mail were worn in conjunction with plated armour for that added protection, particularly for areas plate could not cover, such as arms and the groin. It would have been pretty hot with all that gear on.

Coats of plated armour were later developed, which consisted of a series of plates linked on top of one another. They could withstand high-velocity strikes from a javelin or lance, driven home by somebody charging forwards on horseback. Only the most powerful strikes could pierce such armour.

One of the main defensive strengths of plated armour came from its curved design, which helped to deflect both blades and arrows. As with mail, steel was the best material due to its hardness. This toughness was obtained by heating the steel to extreme temperatures and then submerging it into cold water, a process known as 'quenching'. You may have seen steelworkers doing this after forging the likes of blades and horseshoes.

Once quenched, the steel was re-heated to make it more resilient. Heating to the perfect temperature was key. In pre-thermometer times this was difficult, as you can imagine, so instead, armourers observed the colour of the heated steel. When heated, steel turns from yellow to brown, to blue, to red. Once blue, it is quenched a second time, permanently fixing its hardness. Arrows will bounce off steel crafted in such a way—unless from close range, as we discussed in the last chapter.

Wearing a suit of armour was like being in your own private world. The senses were deadened: sight limited, sound muffled, breathing stifled (depending on the type of helmet). It would have been extremely warm too. But it provided an odd sense of security. Fully geared up, you were a walking fortress.

With all that armour, it's often assumed the medieval knight was immobile. Not quite. Each suit of armour was tailored to the individual. The aim was not to cause any impediment to movement. A warrior had to fight the enemy, and to fight his armour as well would be too distracting. The pieces of armour around the vital organs—the chest and head—were thicker and heavier than those on the arms and legs to try and reduce weight as much as possible.

Armour, therefore, wasn't that heavy—a suit of armour weighed approximately 50 pounds, which is around 3 to 4 stone. If a knight fell from a horse, he could quite easily pick himself up, not get stuck on the ground like a tortoise knocked on its shell.

The appearance of armour was a big deal for knights. Chest plates had grand etchings. Pauldrons, gauntlets, and even leg armour were fashioned into elaborate designs. Other pieces were enamelled and finished with a fine trim. It was very much a way to make a statement.

Leather Armour

A few brief points on the type of armour that dominated before the wave of metal that followed.

Leather was cheap and simple to make and easy to maintain—many soldiers could make repairs to it themselves. The materials were easy to come by too, i.e. from the hides of animals. Often leather was crafted into coats and jackets which could help block blows from enemies.

Leather could be boiled to provide extra hardness. This type of armour was known as Cuir bouilli. It wasn't boiled in water, mind, but in vats of oil or molten wax. It was then shaped into the likes of breastplates, coats of scales, gauntlets, vambraces and greaves. Cuir Bouilli did not, however, fare well in bad weather, with water cracking and rotting it.

Another form of leather armour that developed was to stitch small metal plates to a leather jacket, in essence creating a suit of scales. A more resilient form than just a coat of leather.

So there we have a few of the basics of medieval armour. There are different types of armour from all over the world that haven't been covered and they're well worth checking out. Use this as a starting point, a base, and branch out far and wide. Next, we'll look at ways of getting through all this armour.

III. Weapons

Swords, shields, spears... they feature in the vast majority of fantasy stories. To write about them with confidence you must first know a bit about them, and that's what this chapter aims to deliver—a whistle-stop tour of the most common weapons of the European Middle Ages.

The development of weapons in the Middle-Ages resulted from the advancement in armour. The trusty sword was no match for the walking tanks that were armoured knights, unable to pierce, smash or crack the steel plates they covered themselves with. In fact, a shortsword, thrust at arm's length with both hands, could puncture plated armour by a mere inch—and chances were the blade would get stuck. So weaponsmiths the world over went back to the workshop to devise weapons to defeat the armoured warrior. Let's take a look at some of the things they came up with.

Falchion

This weapon has cropped up before when we looked at archery. The falchion was a singled edged blade, around 24 to 30 inches long and weighing around 5 to 8 pounds, which is a little lighter than a large bag of sugar.

It was designed to combine the technique of a sword with the weight of an axe, which made it an effective weapon against the likes of chain mail, which it could cleave right through. When faced against plated armour, however, it ran into sticky ground. Like the shortsword, the blade would lodge into the armour, and a wielder unable to yank it free would present his armoured foe with a glorious opportunity to land a telling blow.

Broadsword

Also referred to as the basket-hilted sword, this was a blade that had a broad base before narrowing into a wicked, sting-like point. It required a skilled and practised wielder, and a skilled bladesmith too—such designs required the finest steel crafted in the right way, otherwise there was a good chance the metal would shatter in combat.

The purpose of the basket-hilted cross guard was to give some protection to the hand. Some had fancy designs and others were simple, serving their purpose without any frills.

The broadsword inspired the development of a blade known as the **estoc**, also known as the **English tuck**. This lengthy blade had a signature cruciform hilt and required two hands to wield. It lacked any sharp edges and instead possessed a sharp point designed to pierce armour. It was merely a thrusting weapon which became impractical in the heat of close combat.

The estoc holds similarities to the rapier and sabre, both weapons more at home in the realm of fencing than on the battlefield.

Mace

One of the ways to defeat plated armour was by crushing it, and there was arguably no better way to do that than with a mace. It developed from the crude yet effective wooden club and was, at one time, favoured by priests who preferred weapons that did not draw blood (but crushed skulls instead. Yeah, real holy, fellas.)

The mace came in a variety of styles and sizes. Some were spherical or oval, covered in spikes or ribs. They tended to be made from steel, weighing between 4 and 6 pounds, which is about the weight of a table lamp—lighter than you think.

A blow to an unarmoured foe would be lethal, and against plate would certainly cause a concussion, bruising, or even haemorrhaging. It was designed for close, aggressive combat, used in accompaniment with a shield. It could even deflect blows from swords, though this was tricky.

A mace on its own wouldn't be enough to kill a well-armoured warrior. Knocking the enemy to the ground was the aim so they could be finished off quickly with a dagger through the visor, eye slit, or weak spot, such as behind the knees, armpit, under the breastplate or if you're a cruel bastard, the groin.

The flail

Similar to the mace, the flail was also a weapon inspired by its cruder predecessors. It was an ancient agricultural tool, consisting of a wooden club hinged by rope or chain to a wooden staff, sort of like a nunchuck. Some sadistic prick decided to replace the club with a spiked ball, and voilà, you have yourself a killing machine.

In the medieval military world, it became known as the ball and chain, and many variations were developed, the most common being a single-handed weapon with a handle about 3 feet in length and a reach of around 2 to 4 feet. At the base of the staff was a chain to wrap around the wrist. It had the nickname 'The Holy Water Sprinkler' (those priests at it again). Some variations even had two or even three spiked balls at the end.

This was a dangerous weapon, not just for a foe, but for the wielder too. The wielding arm had to remain extended at all times, and that ball had to keep on swinging—the higher the speed the easier it was to control, paradoxically.

Coming up against it must have been terrifying, with one eye on the spiked ball flashing left and right, and the other eye on the wielder. It did, however, make for a rubbish defensive weapon, unable to deflect blows, and if the swinging stopped for a moment, your foe had a chance to attack. It was bloody exhausting to use too.

Warhammer

This weapon was also inspired by a cruder predecessor, in this instance the wooden mallet. The warhammer had two different features: a flat head—the hammer side if you will—which with some variations had serrations to bite into armour, and; the other side which consisted of a long narrow spike, known as 'The Crow's Beak', designed to puncture plate.

It was light enough to carry one-handed, most effective in quick combinations—a blow to stun with the hammer, followed by a ruthless puncture.

As with all weapons designed to pierce armour, the wielder often had one chance to land the killing blow. If the point became lodged the foe had a nice opportunity to strike back. Killing is never straightforward, is it?

Spears

The spear is perhaps the oldest weapon of human making and it's fair to say, it's stood the test of time. It was a favourite of the Greeks, Romans and Persians, used to great effect in phalanx's and shield walls. When it came up against thick, plated armour, its effectiveness began to wane. The points lacked the sharpness to pierce and couldn't generate enough power to penetrate.

The Medieval Germans sought to tackle these problems when they developed an interesting weapon called the **ahlspiess,** which translates to the 'eel spear.' It was around five feet long and weighed between 8 and 10 pounds. It consisted of a sharp point at the end of a slender blade, with a cross guard and wooden haft.

With this weapon, the wielder could aim for weak spots in armour, or pierce right through it. The downside was that it was pretty heavy, with all the weight at the business end, and it required two-hands, so defensive options were limited.

If you want to learn more about fighting with spears, I recommend reading the Killer of Men series by Christian Cameron. It's an historical fiction series about the Greek/Persia wars from the perspective of the Greeks, who were renowned for their use of the shield and spear in their tactical formation, the phalanx.

Billhook

We come to probably my favourite of all these means of killing: the billhook.

As with a lot of weapons, the billhook began its life as an agricultural tool, one that's still used today. It consisted of a long, single-edged blade with a curved end, and a spike branching off it. At the back of the blade was another, smaller spike, known as a fluke. It was around 6 to 8 feet long and weighed around 10 pounds.

This weapon provided flexibility in the attack, able to thrust, slash and deflect. Perhaps the most effective feature was its ability to hook onto armour. This enabled the wielder to pull or push armoured foes off balance. It was capable of deadly combinations with the top spike able to pierce plate if used with enough force. The fluke at the back was also used for stabbing. The billhook was also very effective against cavalry, able to sweep riders from their saddles.

The downside was it required two hands, so quick feet and the ability to parry were important to make up for the lack of a shield. If a blow was blocked, it had to be swept away. It was also pretty useless against thrusting blows.

Shields

When you think of a shield you think of its ability to block projectiles and blows, but in fact, it was quite an effective weapon.

Shields have been around for over 4,000 years, still used today by the police. Over the course of this period they've had to contend with lots of different weapons—arrows, javelins, throwing axes, heavier Dane axes, maces, swords, petrol bombs ... the list could go on.

Two qualities are necessary from a shield: strength and lightness. To achieve this magic combination in the Middle Ages, a variety of materials were used. One of the earliest was linden wood. This material is extraordinarily light and flexible. Linden shields were held together with a glue made from cheese. Unsurprisingly, they didn't last long in battle, shattering when struck by arrows, or any blow for that matter. But it tasted alright.

To achieve extra strength, linden shields were wrapped in the untreated hide of a cow—it had to be from a cow, which is much tougher than that of a sheep, for example. This did, however, add a fair bit of weight but could absorb blows from projectiles. Against heavier attacks, they were likely to shatter.

The shape of a shield was important to its strength. A lenticular shape—like the lens of an eye—provided the flexibility a shield needed to prevent it from shattering. Other shapes included much smaller, circular shields, known as a buckler. It was used almost as an extension of the wrist, useful for deflecting blows rather than blocking them head-on. It could also be used as a steel fist.

The shield wall

We return to the shield wall, perhaps one of the most effective strategies in military history. It was capable of being taught to individuals with no military experience in a short space of time and proved difficult to break down. It was the go-to formation to for withstanding the charge of an onrushing foe.

A line of warriors stood abreast with shields interlocked, one overlapping the other. If someone tried to pull a shield forwards it wouldn't move, because it meant having to pull a load of other shields too. It did, however, require incredible teamwork. If a single gap in the wall appeared, the floodgates opened and men were open to slaughter. To counter this, it was important for those in the ranks behind to be ready to step in to plug any gaps. There were different tactics for the shield wall. A straight line could be adopted, though this was vulnerable to flanking manoeuvres and cavalry charges. To counter this, the line could be moved into lines or ranks. The denser the formation the harder it was for the enemy to punch through.

A tactic to defeat the shield wall was known as the 'Boar's Snout'. This involved a narrow charge into one section of the wall, pushed forwards by the those rushing behind. The idea was to burst open the wall like a blister.

IV. Castles and Keeps

Fantasy is full of dramatic moments involving castles, keeps, and fortified cities. David Gemmell's *Legend* tells the story of the siege of a city with fabled defensive fortifications by the most powerful army in the land. Two of the most iconic battles in *The Lord of the Rings* series came in *The Two Towers* with Helms Deep and at Minas Tirith in *The Return of the King*. Fans of Game of Thrones will recall the Battle of Blackwater Bay and Daenerys's conquest across the Narrow Sea.

It's the author's knowledge of these defensive structures and how they affect the course of battle which makes these moments so memorable. What challenges do the besiegers' face? What steps must be taken to overcome those challenges? And what must the defenders do to resist, if anything at all?

A brief history

The Middles Ages lasted about a thousand years, kicking off in or around the 5th century and lasting until the 15th. It can be split into two periods: the 'Dark Ages', which ran from 5th to 10th century, and the High Middle Ages, from the 10th to 15th. (I understand the phrase Dark Ages is no longer accepted by some, but for ease, it'll serve here).

Castles didn't really exist in the Dark Ages. What did exist were the remains of Roman fortifications, but only in Western

Europe. Everywhere else structures tended to be made from wood.

Then the High Middle Ages came about and so too "The Age of Castles." You couldn't move for a castle in Europe. There were so many that no historian has been able to comprehensively document them all. Castles were status symbols, a means for the nobility to challenge their king, and incredibly, many continue to exist today.

Useful terms

Here's a quick glossary on fortifications:

Castle: a fortification of the High Middle Ages, characterised by high walls with towers and usually a moat. Served both residential and/or administrative purposes. Large castles were around 20 to 30 meters by 15 to 25 meters, with walls 2 to 4 meters thick.

Fort: a small strongpoint occupied by military personnel.

Citadel: a word used to refer to either a castle or a fortified section within a city. Similar to a castle in size.

Fortress: also referred to as a fortified city or town, it has many features in common with a castle, such as high walls, gatehouses, and battlements, though much larger and housing a populace.

Donjon: a great tower or innermost keep of a castle. The term donjon was later replaced with **keep**.

Rampart: a defensive wall of a castle or walled city, having a broad top with a walkway and typically a stone parapet.

Portcullis: a strong, heavy grating that can be lowered into grooves in the ground. Usually found in gatehouses.

In addition to these main types of fortification, there were **tower houses**, **observation posts**, **fortified churches** and **monasteries**.

Early fortifications

Castles evolved out of early, cruder fortifications, three in particular: the gród, the bergfried, and the motte and bailey.

The **gród** was a simple, circular fortification that consisted of an earthen rampart with wooden walls, a fortified gate, and sometimes a moat.

The **bergfried** was a tower, used as lookout posts and later as residences. Before the 13th century, they were mostly made of wood. Entrances to bergfrieds were found on the first floor instead of the ground floor. The reason? Bergfrieds and keeps tended to serve as the last point of defence and having it a floor higher allowed for ladders or platforms to be pulled up, making it more difficult for the enemy to get inside.

The **motte and bailey** consisted of a wooden tower standing upon a man-made mound, also known as a motte. The motte was located within a courtyard known as a bailey, which itself was encircled by a fence of wooden stakes (also known as a palisade), with a fortified gate. It was a popular fortification with the Vikings.

Towers

Towers played an integral role in the defence of a fortification. When constructed as part of the wall, they jutted forward to allow for flanking fire. They were also constructed as stand-alone forts. In early years they were made from wood, and later, stone.

In most instances towers were placed at corners of walls but were also added at intervals, sometimes at set distances, others random. It all depended on the terrain, available resources, and the skill of the builder. These factors also influenced the height of a tower.

A clever feature seen in some towers was to have an open back. Not only did it allow for supplies to easily be hauled up, but if that tower was overrun by attackers, the open back prevented the attackers from using it against the defenders. Some towers were cut off from the wall by drawbridges for added defence.

Early towers were square in shape and the dead angles made them vulnerable to mining attacks, i.e. the enemy digging underneath the walls and bringing them down, a process known as undermining. In the 12th century, more circular or semi-circular towers were introduced to combat this. This was a risk the Romans were already aware of and is why many Roman fortifications had D-shaped towers.

Staircases inside towers and battlements turned clockwise to allow for the defenders to fight with their right hand and restricting the swing of any attacker. Uneven steps were also employed to stumble and stagger attackers as they tried to ascend.

Gatehouses, moats and drawbridges

The gatehouse was perhaps the most important feature of a fortification; in theory, it was the easiest point of access for attackers. As a result, more effort was spent on defending this point than any other, leading to a number of cunning and cruel features to repel any besiegers.

Gatehouses consisted of a set of reinforced wooden and/or metal doors and a portcullis made of reinforced wood or iron. An example of a mighty gatehouse can be seen in Harlech Castle in Wales. It had three portcullises, three doors, and four towers. If you managed to get past the first you were trapped at the second, and so on. The walls of the gatehouse were punctuated with arrow slits through which the defenders could fire upon the attackers, and murder holes in the ceiling through which arrows could be fired, rocks dropped or hot liquids poured.

One simple yet effective feature of gates was to place them at an angle instead of facing forwards. The purpose was to prevent battering rams having a clear charge. Another feature designed with this in mind was the barbican, which was an outcropping of the wall in front of the gatehouse, again designed to obstruct the path of any attackers.

Drawbridges were basic in construction, raised by chains and winches. They went hand in hand with moats, so if there was no moat, there was no drawbridge. The moat is one of the oldest features of fortifications. Simply put, it was a ditch surrounding the castle or keep. Rivers, lakes, ponds, or swamps were used to fill them, others were dry.

A moat had to be deep enough to prevent an attacker from wading through it and wide enough to stop someone from leaping across. Around 3 meters, or 9 feet, was the average depth before the 11th century. After that, they grew much deeper. The size of the moat, however, depended on the terrain and how easily it could be excavated.

Moats were also reinforced with other obstructions, such as sharp stakes along the bottom, walls and bank. A deep moat also protected against the threat of undermining.

One thing about moats to keep mind is that they tended to be disgusting. Excrement and waste from the fortification were often tossed into the water, turning them into foetid cesspools. It was the job of the peasantry to clean it up, on average twice per year. A shitty job if ever there was one.

Walls

The phrase **enceinte** is the technical term for the walls and towers that encircled a fortification (it's also an archaic word for pregnant). The outermost walls were also referred to as curtain walls.

Walls developed significantly during the Middle Ages. One of the earliest types of wall was a dense structure made of earth and wood. Timber walls soon replaced these, though they were thin, vulnerable to fire, and over time, decayed. The solution to such problems came in the form of stone walls, though early stone walls were pretty thin too.

The Roman method of building walls was much superior. They built two walls with a space in between which they filled with rubble. Despite Roman walls surviving into the Middle Ages, nobody thought to copy them. Arrogance, perhaps? Or maybe ignorance?

So how big were walls? It's hard to say. Few records were kept of the constructions of walls, so what's known today is the result of archaeology and guestimates. We can turn again to the Romans who had a pretty good system for making walls. For every one meter of height, there had to be 0.25 meters width. So, for example, a wall 6 meters high would be 1.5 meters thick. But it all depended on how thick the walls *needed* to be. Vulnerable sections of wall were built the thickest, whereas those upon favourable terrains, such as hills, were thinner.

Towers became a staple feature of walls, ranging in height from 10 meters to as tall as 37 meters. Toward the end of the Middles Ages, the height of some walls was raised to the height of towers.

Battlements

A battlement, also known as a parapet, is an encompassing term for the upper part of a fortified wall. A battlement was made up of crenels (an indentation in the wall), embrasures (an opening in the wall), and merlons (the solid part of a crenellated parapet between two embrasures).

Merlons were not always rectangular in shape. In time they became more decorative, the style influenced by region and culture. In the Middle-East for example, the shape of merlons was influenced by Islam.

If the walls weren't very high it left the defenders in range of attacking archers. To counter this, the spaces in between merlons sometimes featured wooden shutters. This did, however, restrict the archer's range of fire to what was just beneath them. As the skills of masons developed, these shutters became redundant. Instead, slits known as **arrow loops** were carved into the stone through which arrows could be fired. At first, they were thin, restricting the scope of fire to one direction, but over time wedge-shaped variations developed. A cross-shaped loop was one such variation which allowed archers to shoot left and right. A feature called an oillet—a small circular observation hole—was also added.

Behind the crenels was the wall walk, also known as an **allure**. In some castles they were built into the walls, in others they were wooden, supported by beams. Towers, which often were incorporated into the battlements, also had allures, giving defenders greater height with which to observe the battle and target threats. Towers with no allures had roofs of slate or lead, often conical in shape.

To get up and down the allures two options were preferred: the bog standard ladder, or a stairway within a wall or tower. The latter was more effective defensively. If attackers swarmed upon the walls, they became trapped, exposed, unless they managed to take a tower.

To aid the defenders further, in or around the 12th century a feature known as **hoardings** was developed. They were wooden structures which projected out over the wall, sort of like scaffolding. This protruding scaffolding allowed for a greater range of fire and crucially, a vantage point that hung over those below, allowing the defenders to drop rocks and scorching liquids like pitch. Hoardings were vulnerable to fire, but to counter this they were covered with wet hides. Hoardings were later incorporated into the walls and in their floors were **machicolations**, the fancy word for murder hole.

Windows were a rare feature on towers and walls and even in keeps. They were seen as weak points. Only residential towers or keeps had windows, which were made from glass, normal or stained, or just iron bars (glass was expensive).

Inside the walls

What did the defenders need to sustain themselves? One of the most important features was a well. Rainwater could be gathered too, but without a supply of water, defenders couldn't last long. Water was also vital for dousing any fires caused by attacks.

Residential areas were usually found in a keep or tower. Inside was a great hall or banqueting room, bedrooms, garderobe (toilet), storage rooms. The kitchen was kept separate due to the risk of fire.

A classic feature of the great hall is a huge hearth. It wasn't until the 14th century that chimneys were introduced, so up until that time people were exposed to toxic fumes. Walls, particularly in the great hall, were decorated with tapestries, which provided some insulation. With few windows, illumination came from torches held in sconces and candles.

The courtyard, or bailey, was the main open area within a castle. Some larger castles had more than one courtyard. Other buildings you'd find within a castle were a chapel, stables, and barracks. Castles did not have dungeons during the Middle Ages. Prisoners were kept in towers; only in the Renaissance period were prisoners moved to the pits of the castle.

V. The Siege

Helms Deep, Dros Delnoch, Minas Tirith. The sieges of these fantasy cities are some of the most iconic in the genre. A lot goes into a siege logistically and tactically, meaning a sound understanding of defensive structures and attacking methods is important when it comes to writing about them. That's what this chapter aims to do—arm you with the tools to build walls and then tear them down.

The development of fortifications and the development of siege tactics are inextricably linked. It seems to be human nature that if someone builds a wall, someone else wants to tear it down. The best way to explore such tactics is to work our way through a siege from the perspective of the attackers.

Moats

The first obstacle any attacker would have to overcome is the moat (if there is one). If the moat was small and shallow it could either be jumped across or planks placed over it to make walkways. Any bigger and it had to be filled in. If it was a water-filled moat, that water first had to be drained out, and one way of doing so was by digging drainage holes or channels around the moat and then connecting them together. Rocks, dirt, wood, or whatever else the attackers could get a hold of were used to fill in the moat. Remember, while all this manual labour was going on, the defenders were peppering them with darts of death.

The battering ram

Moat dealt with, next came the gate and walls. One of the oldest but most efficient methods of getting through a gate was by using a battering ram—a heavy log or tree trunk. A battering ram carried by men alone was sufficient to get through small gates, but larger gates required something a bit more robust.

Enter the **cat,** a carriage in which a battering ram was hung and then swung at the gate. It was also known as the mouse, weasel, and sow. To increase the strength of the ram it was banded with iron rings and reinforced with an iron head to stop it from shattering. Cats were often covered with wet hides to protect the ram operators from projectiles and fire. Instead of a ram, some cats had an iron pole attachment which was used to chisel away at the mortar of the walls. Mortar gave the walls strength, but if it failed it left the piled stones, often of differing sizes, vulnerable to collapse. Cats were also used without a ram to provide a safe space for siege engineers to go about undermining the walls or filling in moats.

To counter these cats, the defenders used a few cunning tactics. The easiest one was to smash them to bits with heavy rocks. Another tactic adopted by the Muslims in the Levant, and adopted later by the Crusaders, was to try and hook the ram and flip it over.

The good old ladder

The quickest, most direct and straightforward approach to overcoming the walls and gate was to scale them with ladders. You've no doubt seen depictions of this tactic and it's fair to say it's a touch dangerous, and in some cases suicidal. With no protection save the armour on their backs and the cover of friendly archers, attackers had to rush up the rungs and drive back the awaiting defenders, all the while dealing with the risk of the ladder being dislodged and pushed backwards. Ladders fell out of favour when the height of walls was increased.

Siege towers

To compete with growing walls, the attackers needed another way of taking the battlements. The solution was the siege tower, also known as the belfry. This siege engine has ancient roots beyond the Middle Ages but featured heavily during The Age of Castles. It consisted of a wooden tower built on wheels. Inside were several levels which the attackers could ascend.

The top level usually consisted of a drawbridge which could be lowered onto the battlements. Some had a level above this which provided a platform for attacking archers to shoot at those upon the battlements. And some towers even had a battering ram on the bottom level. Three birds stoned at once.

The siege tower did have weaknesses. Being wooden it was susceptible to fire, which is why they were usually covered in wet hides. One type of fluid used to wet the hides was urine, something that wasn't in short supply on the battlefield. The transportation of siege towers was also tricky. Given their shape they were prone to toppling when on uneven ground, which was tricky when faced with moats or inclines.

It was imperative to the success of a siege to pin down the defenders with archery and missile fire which allowed the siege equipment to advance. Attackers set up contraptions called mantlets, which were wooden shields held upright by beams, around 2m by 2m, to allow archers to provide covering fire.

Mining

One of the main tactics adopted to bring down a wall, and perhaps the most dangerous yet effective, was mining. Under the protection of cats and hefty shields, miners used picks and other tools to destabilise walls.

Moats made mining difficult. One of sufficient depth could dissuade even the most ambitious of miners, but shallower moats could be dug underneath. Reaching the foundations of the wall, the miners filled the tunnel with flammable objects and set it afire. The tunnel supports collapsed in the heat, collapsing the tunnel and the ground above. So too went the base of the wall.

The defenders had methods for detecting when a mine was being dug. They used the Jurassic Park method of watching a bowl of water for ripples. To defend against mines they dug counter-mines to collapse those of the attackers, smoked them out, or sent down troops to kill the diggers before ending the threat by collapsing the mine. Fighting in these confined, pitch black tunnels was claustrophobic, frantic and brutal.

Projectiles

There were a number of projectile-hurling siege weapons used in the Middle Ages, each with its strengths and limitations.

Crafted in the Roman era, the **ballista** was a giant crossbow. A single bolt could cleave through groups of men, though it wasn't much use against stone walls.

There was the **catapult** too, also known as the mangonel, which consisted of a wooden beam with a bowl at one end, usually filled with rocks. The beam was winched down and released to spring the contents of the bowl forwards. Projectiles from catapults had a low velocity and usually weren't heavy enough to cause significant damage. It had a range of about 500 meters, beyond the reach of archers. Catapults were used in groups, or batteries, to target sections of wall or defensive positions. Using them in such clusters caused massive damage.

The **trebuchet** was similar to the catapult but instead of a bowl, it had a sling in which projectiles could be loaded and hurled. It was better able to throw heavier missiles than the catapult—as heavy as 150 kilograms, which is about the weight of a panda. Yes, a panda. It operated much like the modern day mortar, low velocity but a high trajectory, and it was much more accurate and destructive than the ballista or catapult. It had a range similar to the catapult, if not a little greater.

One of the latterly adopted siege weapons of the Middles Ages was the cannon. In the 14th century, the technology was in its infancy so they were small and ineffective against walls. It was only in the 16th century did they become a force to be reckoned with.

The medieval cannon was made of cast iron or bronze (both were used in the early days) using similar techniques to how they made bells. These early cannons weren't very big—historians estimate about three feet in length—with the bottleneck end wide enough to hold the shaft of an arrow. To ignite it, a hot iron was held to a trail of powder which fed into the bowl-shaped chamber and then to the charge.

These early cannons had various names. *Pot-de-fer* was one such name, which in French means iron pot. In Italy, it was known as the vasi, which means vase. Early cannons had no carts or wheeled platforms. Forget about aiming. With nothing to hold it down, the cannon would have shot up into the air upon firing, sending projectiles in indiscriminate directions. But one thing cannons brought in those early days was fear. Never had anyone seen anything could make such thunderous and terrifying noises. In 1346 French historian, Francois Mezeray, noted in his account of the Battle of Crecy that King Edward "struck terror into the French Army with five or six pieces of cannon, it being the first time they had seen such thundering machines." They may have been ineffective at inflicting damage, but the method had been cracked and over the years the designs improved.

The breakthrough seemed to come around 1377. Philip the Bold, Duke of Burgundy, commissioned the construction of a monster cannon, one which could fire a ball weighing four hundred and fifty pounds. It was reported to have taken nine men nine days to build and was tested at the Siege of Odruik. Medieval author, Jean Froissart, reveals how it fared:

> "The castle of Odruik was situated on a motte, surrounded by a ditch filled with very large spikes … The Duke of Burgundy set up his cannons and fired maybe five or six quarrels in order to provoke surrender. Three quarrels were such that, because of the power of the discharge, they penetrated the walls."

'The power of the discharge' referred to relates to gunpowder. While it may have offered great rewards on the battlefield, it brought with it many risks. In the early days, for instance, the composition of saltpetre, charcoal and sulphur was merely mixed together and tossed into the cannon with nothing to keep it together. It led to irregular ignitions and fires sparking after the explosion. Plus, saltpetre was expensive. This problem was solved however when some clever chap came up with the idea of 'corning'. The mixing process was altered so instead the powders were wetted to make a paste. This was then spread out into a thin cake and left to dry. It was a game-changer. The ingredients held together, it was easier to transport, easier to load into a cannon, and above all, led to more consistent, faster, and violent explosions.

As the years went on the cannon developed, becoming more mobile, more powerful and more reliable and for over two hundred years endured as a key weapon for attackers and defenders alike.

What about the defenders?

What did the defenders have at their disposal? Well, they possessed the same siege weapons as the attackers: ballista, catapults, trebuchets, and cannons. Ballistae were usually placed atop towers and were used to target siege towers and cats, as well as large groups of attackers. Catapults and trebuchets were normally found in courtyards and again used to destroy belfries and such.

Perhaps the most lethal of all weapons was something known as Greek Fire, which has been likened to modern-day napalm, though its ingredients have been lost to time. Probably a good thing. For fans of Game of Thrones, I imagine it's one of the influences behind wildfire. This, as well as other hot liquids such as pitch and oil, were dropped onto attackers to scorch and burn.

VI. The Pesky Peasantry of the Middle Ages

In this chapter we'll explore the lives of the medieval peasantry, a class of people somewhat shrouded in mystery—peasants weren't good note-takers. In exploring the lives of the peasantry we'll uncover what it was like to be one of them, the kinds of places they lived in, and what their day to day lives involved, all with the intention of giving you some nuggets of inspiration for your own fantasy stories.

The medieval peasant

The term peasant is misleading. Although they were at the bottom of the pyramidal feudal system that operated in England during much of the Middle Ages, they were not as brutish and stupid as they're often led to believe. In fact, all that 'peasant' really meant was that you lived mainly off the produce of your own labour and that you were self-sufficient. No different from the allotment keepers and off-the-gridders around the world today. Peasants farmed the land to provide food for everyone else, but often the land did not belong to them, but rather a lord or a baron who loaned them a piece of land in exchange for labour and taxes.

Where better to look for an insight into the life of the peasant than from someone who lived during the era. Here's a quote from 1395 from medieval author Jean Froissart:

> *"It is the custom in England, as with other countries, for the*
> *nobility to have great power over the common people, who*
> *are serfs. This means that they are bound by law and custom*
> *to plough the field of their masters, harvest the corn, gather it*
> *into barns, and thresh and winnow the grain; they must also*
> *mow and carry home the hay, cut and collect wood, and*
> *perform all manner of tasks of this kind."*

But despite this work-orientated account, peasants had quite a lot of control over their lives. Some were chosen to sit on village councils or in local courts to deal with issues ranging from trivial boundary disputes to murders. The lords, in short, couldn't be arsed to get involved in these things. But this worked against them. The peasants grew savvy, learned the laws and how to read and write.

An example of the bright thinking of peasants can be seen in 1200. King John proposed a visit to Nottingham. To get there his route would have taken him through the village of Gotham (not Batman). This meant it'd become a kings highway and as a result, the people would have to pay more taxes. The villagers of Gotham didn't like this, so when the king's messengers arrived the whole village pretended to be insane—madness was considered a contagious illness back then. The king decided on a different route.

A peasant's humble abode

Back in the Middle Ages, a village was known as a 'vill', which in Middle English translated to town. Vills could include small hamlets, scatterings of farms, or compact groups of houses too. The term vill was used to describe a unit of government too, the smallest unit of all.

The shape of houses varied. The Celts, for example, preferred roundhouses, whereas English peasants opted for a cruck house, rectangular in shape with triangular thatched roofs. They were constructed with a wooden frame and panelled with wattle (woven twigs) and daubed with mud. The exterior walls were sometimes plastered with quicklime and earth to give it extra strength, which depending on the type of soil in the area, left the walls with a white, yellow or reddish hue. These early homes lasted little more than twenty or thirty years.

Windows were uncommon and those that did exist lacked glass. Shutters made a poor effort at keeping out draughts. The interior floor was merely compacted earth or was covered with straw.

Most houses consisted of one room, though some had two, and others featured a mezzanine level which usually housed sleeping quarters—the heat rising from the fire below often made it one of the warmest parts of the house.

The central feature was usually a fire. Early houses lacked a chimney so toxic fumes tended to circulate before escaping through cracks in windows or thatch. It was a source of a lot of health problems.

Furniture was basic: wooden benches, stools, tables. For some, chairs were too expensive. Chests were used to store possessions and hooks used for hanging things off the dirty ground. Beds were made from straw.

Peasants weren't the only inhabitants of these houses. If they owned animals—pigs, oxen, chickens—they often lived inside too. If they didn't have a barn, where else were they to go? They were too valuable to risk losing. Outside they could wander off, be preyed upon by the wolves and bears that still roamed the forests of England, or be stolen by reprobates. Just imagine the smells and the mess and the noise, let alone the fleas. A plant called fleabane was used by many peasants in their homes.

Not all peasant houses were like this. Peasants of higher standing, such as the reeve (the village manager) often owned land, had more furniture, and decorative items, such as pottery.

In the later medieval period, particularly after the Black Death when peasants found themselves with a little more coin than before, wattle and daub houses were ditched for brick and timber. In busier and bigger vills you could find them living in townhouses. These were timber framed with two floors. The ground floor was usually used as a shop front or workshop. Livestock was kept in there too. The second floor was used for living. A big reception hallway was characteristic of a wealthy person; it was usually the first impression visitors got of their house. A dining room was another main feature. Up until around the 14th-century, windows tended to be made of brown or green glass. Some townhouses, from around 15th century onwards, had a latrine, which was a very crude toilet. Fancy.

Each vill and city differed, but they tended to have characteristic traits. Most were found on rivers, coasts, or along trade routes. The market was the backbone of a city or town, usually found in squares. Travelling merchants moved from city to city, town to town, selling their goods in these markets. The streets would have been smelly. Faeces and waste were tossed wherever was convenient, i.e. rivers or the streets themselves.

Life as a peasant

What did peasants eat? Pottage was a popular dish, not by choice. Pottage involved taking anything and putting it into a pan of water and allowing it to boil for two hours. Everything had to be boiled because human excrement was used as fertiliser in the fields. Herbs, spices and garlic helped the taste.

There was an instant form of pottage too. Pre-made pottage was made into a sort of bread and taken to the fields. Ale or mead was used to soak and break it up—alcoholic drinks were preferred to water because back then water wasn't very drinkable with all the shit in it. As well as people dumping stuff in water sources, excrement was known to seep from latrine pits—the hole in the ground everyone went the toilet in—and cause fatal contamination.

Peasants didn't bother cleaning themselves much. It was said that a peasant received two baths in their lifetime: once when born and the other when they died. There was no knowledge of hygiene. Compare this to the Romans. They built public baths for the lower classes to use. Enlightened.

Peasants lived well into their sixties, though many died young, a lot not making it past infancy due to disease. One thing they did have was pretty good teeth. Their diets contained little sugar and what they ate was quite coarse in texture which scoured their teeth clean. That said, there's evidence from excavated teeth of huge plaque build ups which would have left deformities of the face.

281 | A Fantasy Writers' Handbook

The lives of peasants did improve, you'll be glad to hear. Those who survived the Black Death found themselves in a peculiar situation—they had the power. With huge swathes of the population gone, there was a high demand for work and that gave the peasantry the power to negotiate better terms. Every cloud.

VII. A Lordly Life

The title of 'Lord' was more of an umbrella term for a number of different classes of nobleman during the Middle Ages. Top of the roster was the king. Then you had dukes, counts, barons, and lastly, knights.

To gain an insight into the role and lives of the lords of the Middles Ages we'll first take a brief look at the reign of King Richard II, otherwise known as Richard the Tyrant. From there we'll turn our focus to the world of barons, the individuals who held almost unlimited power over the land granted to them by the king. In doing so you'll glean some information as to how they lived , which may prove useful when writing your own stories.

King Richard II

A megalomaniac. The first monarch to commission a portrait of himself. A man who regarded himself as a saint. A tyrant who ruled in his own interest. An total nutter. But is that true?

Richard II was crowned in 1367 at the age of just 10 and reigned until 1400. Four years into his rule he had to deal with a peasant revolt. In classic tyrannical fashion, he rode out to meet the peasants and pardoned them all because of his *'abhorrence for the shedding of civil blood.'*

After this, he took the rather unconscionable step in seeking to end the expensive war with France which was crippling England's taxpayers, i.e. the poor. And this was the thing that pissed off his subjects the most. Well, the subjects that held power: the barons. They hated everything about Richard, from his wife to his policy of peace with France.

See, war was the main way the barons made money. As we'll learn in more detail below, the barons had total control over the levels of taxation they could set for those residing on their land. And war meant higher taxes, an excuse to plunder the limited wealth of the peasants they were charged to look after.

In response, a handful of barons overthrew Richard, but he regained power in mere days. Instead of executing his rebellious barons, he exiled them, one of whom was Henry IV. Years later Henry returned from exile, threw Richard into gaol, and seized the throne for himself.

Henry ordered the chroniclers—the monks and writers who recorded the histories of the time—to alter their texts to defame Richard, which is why this seemingly great king is now known as a tyrant. It sounds like something from Orwell's *1984*.

Barons

So who were these powerful, rebellious barons?

The king owned all the land in the country. He did not sell it off, rather leased it. And the individuals who he leased it to were his barons. Most barons started off in a lowly role, such as knights, political advisers, or even ordinary individuals.

These were the people the King felt he could trust to maintain his land, look after those living on it, supply fighting men in times of war, and pay taxes and dues to the exchequer (the royal bank). These parcels of land were known as fiefs, and the barons held complete dominion and jurisdiction over them.

Barons lived in manors—grandiose abodes at the heart of their estate. Living on the land with them were peasants and knights who they loaned the land to. Barons made their coin from the produce of the land, court fines, but mainly from taxes.

The baron acted as arbiter in disputes between peasants and others residing on their land, though as we saw in the above chapter, it was the peasants who tended to carry out most of these administrative affairs, which the barons deemed boring.

It was the role of the baron to monitor harvests and supplies, manage finances such as taxes, rents, and dues. If he was pretty shite at doing any of this, there was a chance the king could confiscate his land. But as we saw above with Richard II, it wasn't so easy for the king to exert his influence over these barons, who enjoyed almost unlimited power over their fiefs.

With coin flowing and coffers swelling, barons began to spend more on artistic pursuits, such as music, paintings, and literature. They sought more types of entertainment too, hiring jesters, minstrels, acrobats, actors, and dancers.

With such wealth, food was of no issue to the baron. A baron was always served before everyone else. Their diets were rich in meat. They ate vegetables too, mostly peas, beans, and onions, and enjoyed quality bread. They drank ale made of hops and mead made from fermented honey and enjoyed wines imported from southern Europe where grapes grew.

The way a baron ate varied depending on their wealth. Rich barons ate off plates and bowls of pewter, whereas poorer barons used wooden plates and bowls. Forks did not exist during the Middle Ages, though knives and spoons did. Most people ate with their fingers and washed their hands in something known as a finger bowl.

What did barons wear? The best money could buy, obviously. Velvets, furs, and silks of scarlet and purple, with gold embroidery. The law even reserved certain fabrics and colours for the nobility, which came about after peasants began to dress in more colourful and flamboyant ways. This occurred after the Black Death when demand for workers soared, empowering the peasants to negotiate better rates of pay with barons who were desperate for people to work the land.

As with lords and ladies in the UK today, the title of baron was a hereditary one. The children of barons were educated by tutors in various languages, literature, history, law, and outdoor pursuits like horse riding, hunting, and hawking, all in preparation for the day they took over.

So this was the life of a baron in a nutshell. They enjoyed unlimited power over their fiefs and those that resided within it, and their influence even extended over their king. I hope this has given you something of an insight into their role during the Middle Ages and perhaps sparked a few ideas you can use in your own fantastical tales!

Part Three: When The Writing Is Done
(If indeed, it ever is...)

Introduction

So here we are, Part Three. The writing is done, the editing complete, if indeed such a thing is ever possible. What now? You want the world to read your story, of course, and hopefully make some cash in the process.

Before you go Googling publishers, there are a few things you can do to help take full advantage of every little opportunity that presents itself along the way. Things that I wished I would have known when I started out. In this section, we'll look at the foundation blocks of your writing career—making a website and what to put on it, building a following, marketing your work, formatting your work for publication, finding publishers, writing cover letters, and some marketing methods for promoting your work.

There's much to cover so let us tarry no more.

The Website: A Writer's Shop Window

If a reader wants to learn more about you and your writing the first thing they're going to look for is your website. In essence, it's a writer's shop window, a place to display your wonderful writing with the hope of intriguing and luring in fans. In not having a website you run the risk of spurning precious opportunities to connect with potential followers, and in a field as competitive as this, you need to take advantage of everything that presents itself.

Making a website

The websiteless writer has a wealth of options available to them, and many of them free. In fact, on my website, you can find a detailed guide to making a website compiled by web developer Robert Mening. Rob's invested a hell of a lot of time signing up for various websites and testing them thoroughly and he gives an honest account of each and every one.

Me, I went for WordPress. I chose it because at the time it was one of the only ones I knew of, it was free, and it required no coding skills, of which I have none. If you're more of a coding boss then you could look to buy your own domain name for a one-off fee and build it yourself. Or you can get someone else to do it for you, but that costs monies.

If you're making your first foray into the online world I'd recommend the free option. No risks. With the likes of WordPress, you can make a decent-looking website quickly and with few headaches. WordPress does all the coding for you, it's easily customisable, and there are plenty of easy to use guides to help you. Your URL will feature '.wordpress.com' but for a nominal fee, you can ditch it.

What to put on it

This is your piece of the web to showcase who you are and what you're about. A modest **about me** page is always a good starting point. You can write this in the first or third person. I prefer the first person. I feel the third is quite distant. You want to make connections with your readers on a personal level and first person helps achieve this. Talk about your favourite genres, writers, books, poems, anything. One way to connect with readers is to reveal a few 'interesting' facts about yourself. By interesting I mean embarrassing. So for instance, my middle name is Edward, which means my name is also Dick Ed (Richard/Dick, Edward/Ed). Another option is to put together a short Q&A. If you've ever done something like this for another site or blog, why not use it? If not, you could copy the questions from someone else and answer them. A photo is a nice addition too. It allows readers to put a face to the name.

About me page done, next you're going to want to showcase a bit of your writing. If you've written any short stories or had anything published, make a separate page for each one, publishing the full piece or sharing the link to read elsewhere. If you've published anything at all, include it on your site. It's your virtual showroom. Make it as attractive to look at as possible. Think about images and a nice, readable font in an inoffensive colour.

One of the other important things to include is a **contact** page. I recommend trying to make yourself as approachable as possible, but that's just me. Have your email address on there or a contact form to reduce the likelihood of spam.

Invitations to connect

One of the most important things you're going to want to include on your site is a function for readers to subscribe to your mailing list. Building a mailing list is something you may have heard of before. Statistically, it's been proven to be the most effective method for writers to market their work. Somebody who subscribes has voluntarily given up a piece of their personal information. They're accepting your invitation to connect and stay in touch. When the time comes to sell your books, someone from your list is more likely to buy a copy rather than a Twitter follower merely interested in a follow for follow arrangement.

How do you get readers to subscribe? It's a good question, one I struggled with until I did a bit of research. Besides producing helpful content, offering an incentive of some kind can provide the necessary encouragement. For instance, when you subscribe to my list you receive a flash fiction story, an eBook filled with creative writing tips, lists of publishers and a list of book reviewers.

One thing you can experiment with is a pop-up form. I was dead against them, but I tried it and the results were remarkable. About 70% of all my email subscribers comes via the pop-up. Perhaps they're not as annoying as you think.

One of the best tools for managing a mailing list and creating a popup form is Mailchimp. It's free up to a certain subscriber limit. You can build multiple lists and sort your subscribers into categories to allow for better target marketing. You can build GDPR-compliant sign up and popup forms which automatically add subscribers to your list. And another canny feature is the ability to send automated emails. So for instance, when someone joins your list you can set a trigger so they receive a welcome email delivering all your lovely writing.

***

It took me a while to make the move to make a website. As odd as it may sound, I didn't feel worthy of one. The way I overcame those feelings of doubt and inadequacy was to make myself the best website I could, and over the past few years it has grown and developed into something that at one point I would have sworn against doing. Just remind yourself that you have absolutely nothing to lose and everything to gain.

Blogging

When somebody first suggested blogging to me I told them, in polite terms, to fuck off. I thought it'd be a waste of time—who even still reads blogs? Turns out, a lot of people do. Today, if somebody asked me what I thought about blogging I'd tell them that I should have started sooner, that I should do it more often before reeling off all of the reasons behind why they should do it themselves. In this chapter, we'll look at these very reasons.

Why blog?

People blog for different reasons—an expression of their creativity, for the fun of writing, to highlight a cause, to share their experiences with others. You can pretty much blog about anything you want. And I suppose this is part of the problem when starting out. What in the seven hells am I going to talk about? In that moment you feel as if you know nothing at all.

But ignore that thought, because you do know things. Things that other people don't. Experiences that other people haven't endured. Have confidence in your words, and if you come up with an idea, start writing. One of the best things about blogging is the freedom of it. There aren't any hard and fast rules, no fixed formatting guides, no editor telling you what you can or cannot say or do. There's just you, your keyboard and a blank slate for you to fill.

Being helpful

Earlier on I said you want to showcase your writing to the world. But what if you have none? A blog is an excellent way of changing that. Not only is it a fantastic way of reaching out to fellow readers and writers but it drives traffic to your site.

A blog is a means of helping others. For me, I chose to blog about the things I've learned while studying the craft of writing so that others could benefit too. It's geared toward expanding people's knowledge and skills and helping them to become better writers. If they improve their craft then we all benefit from the better writing and the brilliant ideas they produce, and now, in this crazy era of ours, we need it more than ever. Forget about gains in exchange. It's sad that as humanity grows, we're becoming more insulated as individuals, more focused on the self than on the whole. Those who merely blog about themselves, particularly if they're not *that* interesting, aren't so enjoyable to read. Who cares at the end of the day? I'm so grateful to the bloggers that share their knowledge and experiences for the benefit of others. I've learned so much from them. And now I follow them, read their every post, and buy their books.

When thinking of what type of content to write, think about what kinds of skills you have and experiences you've lived through or any specialist areas of expertise. What have you learned that you can share with the rest of the world? Don't worry if someone else has already done it. You can do it your *own* way.

Are you doing a creative writing course? Have you been to a workshop? Why not share your notes on what you've learned? I once visited a castle, took some pictures and blogged about it, and it ended up being one of the more popular posts on my site. You can blog about anything! So be helpful. You have something to give to the world. We all do.

Consistency

If you're a sufferer of procrastination like myself, then blogging can be tricky. It requires commitment and dedication. Time must be spent thinking of new and original ideas, planning, drafting, editing, formatting, sharing. A single blog post could take weeks or months to write.

In the beginning, it helps to work out how much you want to produce, and how much you physically can. With all the will in the world, there are times in our lives when we're just unable to do the things we yearn to do. Not long ago I decided to increase my rate of blogging to three times per week. With my job, family and friends, it left me with little time to work on my fiction writing. I kept it up for about a month before reducing it back down to once per week. That's been my average for the vast majority of my time blogging. It works for me, and that's what it comes down to: what works for you. Because if you're doing too much, it's going to affect the quality of your content and readers will be able to tell. And besides, you're not going to enjoy it.

I recommend keeping a feasible schedule. Every Tuesday, for instance. Or every Monday or Friday. Schedule your plotting and drafting around it and allow it to become part of your week. Once it becomes routine, it becomes easy.

Promoting your blog

Once you've published your first blog post or you've just finished polishing your shiny new website, you need to get promoting. People have written whole blogs on this point alone. Here are a few of my favourite pointers:

- **Read other people's blogs and engage with them.** The blogging community is incredibly supportive and co-operative. Bloggers love to read each other's blogs. If you take the time to connect by reading posts and leaving a comment, it goes a long way. Chances are that person will go and read your blog, engage with it, maybe share it, getting your blog out to many more people.

- **Guest blogging.** Once you get your foot in the door on the blogging front and you've made a few friends, why not invite a few other bloggers to write a guest post. Likewise, you can ask other bloggers if they're looking for guest writers. You're collaborating to help each other out. It's win-win. I'm always looking for guest writers for my blog so if you're looking for opportunities, please drop me an email.

- **Join writing forums.** In joining writing forums you can make connections with people who appreciate helpful content. Some have rules about self-promotion, which personal blogs fall under, so watch out for those.

- **Use social media.** Twitter and Facebook are the two platforms I use most. I have more joy with Facebook. There are loads of genre-specific writing groups on there filled with people who'll appreciate your content. On Twitter, use hashtags like #amwriting #amwritingfantasy or

#writingtips, to link your content to potential readers. Check out this very helpful article on marketing on Twitter. When posting always bear in mind the time at which you do so. First thing in the morning, say around 9-11am works well, and another peak time for me is around 1-3pm. Most people who read my blog live in the US so 2pm for me is 9am for them.

Making cash

When most people think of blogging they think of pasty teens bashing away at their keyboards in their bedrooms. Few people take it seriously, but I think the times of change are upon us. Blogging is shifting to the forefront of people's sources of information. People are making careers out of it and earning significantly more than most of us.

One of the simplest and most effective ways to make money from blogging, while also promoting your blog, is through Medium. If you've not heard of it before, it's a monetized blogging platform. Some content is free, but others require a subscription in order to read it. And it's through the funds generated by subscriptions that writers get paid. Medium calculates it as fairly as possible: it goes by the number of unique reads and interactions your post gets, if I'm not mistaken, though they do tend to change it up every now and then. There's no limit to what you can earn, and everyone at least earns $3.50 a month.

On Medium you'll find hundreds of magazines on topics ranging from health and travel to mindfulness and creative writing. Some have readerships of hundreds of thousands. And you can write for them. And earn money for doing so.

I cannot profess to be an expert with Medium, but there are plenty about, and if you're serious about giving this a good go, then I encourage you to read as much as you can about how it works and what the most successful bloggers on there do. There are plenty of helpful articles knocking about, mostly on Medium itself. Here are a few quick pointers to get you going:

- Familiarise yourself thoroughly with how Medium works: formatting, presentation, image permissions and most important of all, the Partner Programme. You'll need to enrol in this to make money and select your posts as being available only for subscribers.
- Get your Medium profile up to a good standard with links back to your own platforms.
- Sign up for Smedian, a sister website of Medium (www.smedian.com). On this site, you sign up to write for different magazines on Medium. Once accepted, you'll be able to submit your posts to those magazines on the Medium website.
- Remember to credit all of your images. If there's no source link for an image, a publication is going to reject it outright.

Breeding opportunities

Blogging, in a sense, is a form of networking. Ah, networking. That vague term they bandied about in university. As I've gotten older my understanding of what it means has grown. And indeed, it means opportunity.

I dislike the phrase 'it's who you know, not what you know'. Knowing people, befriending them, helping and supporting them, can open doors, and this in a nutshell, is networking. So when you comment on another bloggers post, that's networking. Easy?

Online Writing Groups

The writing game can be a lonely one, but it doesn't have to be that way. In fact, working with others can improve your writing tremendously. It can be quite tricky finding fellow writers nearby to meet up with, but the internet has made that a whole lot easier. Hundreds, if not thousands of writing groups exist online. No longer do writers have to sit alone in their bedroom reading work aloud to their cat. But it still can be quite difficult to find the correct writing group for you. So here's a list of all those I'm aware of.

Most, you will see, are on Facebook. While it does have its issues, mostly ethical ones, Facebook is still an active hub for writers of all genres. Be sure to check out the group I manage, *The Sci-Fi and Fantasy Writing Collective*, which has grown exponentially over the past few months. I've included a few from Reddit and forums too. If you know of any others, drop me an email!

This is a permanent page on my site under the Writer's Resources section. I update this list as often as I can.

Name of Group	Platform	Genre
The Sci-Fi and Fantasy Writing Collective	Facebook	SFF
Fantasy Writers Support Group	Facebook	Fantasy
AmWritingFantasy	Facebook	Fantasy

The Sci-fi & Fantasy Writers' Guild	Facebook	Fantasy
RPG and Fantasy Writers and Artists Guild	Facebook	Fantasy
Writing Bad	Facebook	All
Fantasy Writers Group	Facebook	Fantasy
Genre Writers (Fantasy, SciFi, Steampunk et al)	Facebook	SFF
Writers Assembled	Facebook	All
Sci-fi & Fantasy Authors & Readers	Facebook	SFF
Writers' Group	Facebook	All
Scifi,Horror,Fantasy, Paranormal,Fiction,true Story etc etc Authors, Lovers	Facebook	Spec Fic
Sci-Fi, Horror, Doomsday, Fantasy, True Story, Action, etc. Writ	Facebook	Spec Fic
Writers Like Writers	Facebook	All
Epic Sci-Fi, Fantasy, Horror Group	Facebook	Spec Fic
Writers Group	Facebook	All
Indie Authors Support Network	Facebook	All
Fantasy & Sci-Fi writers group	Facebook	SFF
Writer's tips and feedback	Facebook	All
Writers For Writers	Facebook	All
Fiction Writing	Facebook	All
One Stop Fiction Authors' Resource Group	Facebook	All
Sci-Fi Readers & Writers	Facebook	SF
Indie Authors International	Facebook	All
Book Promotion Scifi and Fantasy	Facebook	SFF
WE PAW Bloggers	Facebook	All
Author/Publisher/Editor/Book Readers	Facebook	All
Authors, Reviewers, & Book Lovers	Facebook	All
The Indie Writers' Cooperative	Facebook	All
The Sci-Fi, Horror & Fantasy Group	Facebook	Spec Fic
Celebrating Authors	Facebook	All
Writers Helping Writers	Facebook	All
Authors	Facebook	All
The Writers Tribe	Facebook	All

Creative Writing	Facebook	All
Creative Writers Hangout	Facebook	All
Tune Your English	Facebook	All
Indie Authors & Book Lovers	Facebook	All
Fantasy Writers	Facebook	Fantasy
Aspiring Novelists	Facebook	All
Historical Fiction	Facebook	Historical Fiction
Writing Bad Promotions	Facebook	All
Writing tips for beginners	Facebook	All
Passion for Books	Facebook	All
Socially Aware Fantasy Writers	Facebook	Fantasy
Writers' Gathering Group	Facebook	All
Writers and Readers of Speculative Fiction	Facebook	Spec Fic
Science Fiction, Horror, and Fantasy Writers	Facebook	Spec Fic
Science Fiction/Horror/Fantasy Write Inc.	Facebook	Spec Fic
Fantasy Authors Assemble-Fantasy writers group	Facebook	Fantasy
A Speculative Fiction, Science Fiction, Fantasy, Readers & Writers Hang Out	Facebook	Spec Fic
Science Fiction, Fantasy and other genres: learning group	Facebook	SFF
Fantasy & Sci-Fi Fans, Artists, Reader Writers, Filmmakers & Cosplayers	Facebook	SFF
r/fantasywriters	Reddit	Fantasy
r/Fantasy	Reddit	Fantasy
r/Writing	Reddit	All
r/Worldbuilding	Reddit	All
r/SciFi	Reddit	Sci Fi
r/Writers	Reddit	All
r/writingtips	Reddit	All
SFF Chronicles	Forum	SFF

Formatting a Manuscript

Before it comes to sending out your shiny new stories to publishers, it needs to be formatted in the right way. Most publishers state in their submission guidelines how they wish your story to be formatted. Don't ignore this. If you do, it'll demonstrate to the editors that you either don't care enough to take the time to do it or that you haven't read the guidelines. Both will piss them off just as much. **This is the golden rule when it comes to formatting your work.**

A lot of publishers, particularly those based in the US, will ask for your manuscript to be formatted in the Shunn style. Indeed, William Shunn's formatting guidelines have proven so popular they've become something of the default. By that I mean, if a publisher does not state in their guidelines how they'd like your piece formatted, revert to Shunn.

The Shunn style

William Shunn is the chap behind these formatting guidelines, and his short essays on both formatting manuscripts for short stories and novels are freely available over on his website www.shunn.net.

The URL for the short story guide is > https://www.shunn.net/format/story.html

And for novels > https://www.shunn.net/format/novel.html

I encourage you to read both so here I'll cover just the highlights—some of the biggest pet peeves of editors.

Font

Keep it simple. Shunn recommends using either Times New Roman or Courier. Courier is his strong preference because it's monospaced, meaning every character is evenly spaced apart, which makes it easier to detect spelling mistakes. Size 12 font is also recommended.

Line spacing

Often a subject for debate. Shunn recommends double spacing—it's easier to make notes around the text, and for me, I find it easier to read the text and detect any mistakes.

First page

The first page is where you feature your name, contact information and word count, usually positioned at the top left of the page.

***

Some publishers will ask you to format your manuscript in their own 'house' style. It's worth taking the time to follow their guidelines completely. And it's not that much extra work. I usually save another copy of my formatted piece and just make the adjustments. Shunn is, however, the industry standard it seems, so it won't be often that you have to deviate.

Publishers of Short Fantasy Fiction

It can be tedious work researching publishers, but the good news is it's getting easier. A number of websites exist which allow you to search at will for the precise publisher you want. My favourite amongst these websites is Duotrope. For a small subscription of around $4 a month, you get access to a vast database of publishers of short and long fiction, in myriad genres, as well as lists of literary agents. It's well worth checking out, even just for the free trial.

If you want to save your coin, then do not despair. It just involves a little more work, but to save on that work, below you'll find a list of over a hundred publishers of short fantasy fiction. At the bottom, you'll find a short list of flash fiction publishers too. This list is ever growing, and you can find the latest version at www.richiebilling.com. Subscribers to my mailing list can also get a downloadable version. The online version also includes a bit of extra detail on publishers too, namely their estimated response times and whether or not they accept simultaneous submissions. What does that mean, you may be wondering. Let's cover some of the terms you're likely to encounter on your quest for publication.

> *Pro*: A status afforded to publishers by the Science Fiction and Fantasy Writers of America organization. Highest rates of payment made for all accepted submissions.

Semi-pro: Payments awarded for accepted submissions, though lacking the 'pro' status.

Token: A magazine that offers a 'token' in exchange for accepted submissions, for example, a free copy of their issue.

Paid: A magazine that pays for accepted submissions but lacking the 'pro' status.

Non-payment: A magazine that does not offer anything for accepted submissions, save a well-deserved pat on the back.

Simultaneous submission: refers to whether or not you can send the same story to more than one publisher at the same time. Some publishers permit you to do so provided you tell them in your covering letter/email that you've sent it to somebody else.

1,000 words +

Name	Status	Word limit
Abyss & Apex	Pro	10,000
Albedo	Token	8,000
Apex Magazine	Pro	7,500
Beneath Ceaseless Skies	Pro	14,000

Clarkesworld	Pro	16,000
Heroic Fantasy Quarterly	Semi-pro	10,000
Fantasy Scroll Mag	Paid	5,000
Holdfast Magazine	Token	4,000
Inter Galactic Medicine Show	Pro	17,500
Lightspeed	Paid	10,000
The Magazine of Sci-Fi and Fantasy	Pro	25,000
On Spec	Semi-pro	6,000
Pod Castle (audiobook only)	Paid	6,000
Shimmer	Semi-pro	7,500
Strange Horizons	Paid	10,000
Uncanny Magazine	Paid	6,000
Fireside Magazine	Paid	4,000
Aurealis	Semi-pro	8,000
Glittership (audiobook too)	Semi pro	6,000
Helios Quarterly	Semi-pro	1,500
Selene Quarterly	Semi-pro	1,500
Aurora Wolf	Token	5,000
Strange Constellations	Token	7,500
Mithila Review	Token	8,000
Kzine	Paid	8,000
Giganotosaurus	Token	25,000
Aliterate	Pro	8,000
Cosmic Roots and Eldritch Sho	Pro	1,000+
Gamut Magazine	Pro	5,000
Aphelion Webzine	Non-payme	7,500
Cirsova	Semi-pro	7,500
Crimson Streets	Paid	6,000
Electric Spec	Paid	7,000
Expanded Horizons	Paid	6,000

Gathering Storm Magazine	Paid	2,000
Kaleidotrope	Paid	10,000
Lackingtons	Paid	5,000
Leading Edge Magazine	Paid	10,000
Longshot Island	Paid	5,000
Metaphorosis Magazine	Paid	10,000
Mythic Delirium	Paid	4,000
New Myths	Paid	10,000
Golden Fleece Press	Paid	5,000
Sockdolager	Paid	5,000
Space and Time Magazine	Paid	7,500
SQ Mag	Paid	5,000
Tall Tale TV (audiobook only)	Non-payme	3,000
Far Horizons	Non-payme	3,000
British Fantasy Society	Token	5,000
East of the Web	Paid	Not stated
Writer' Forum	Paid	3,000
Not One of Us	Paid	6,000
Bards and Sages	Paid	5,000
Fantasia Divinity	Paid	7,500
Into the Void	Token	Not stated
Asimov's	Pro	7,500
Interzone	Pro	10,000
The Future Fire	Paid	10,000
Timeless Tales	Paid	2,000
Riddled With Arrows	Paid	1,500
Mad Scientist Journal	Paid	8,000
Hyperion & Theia	Paid	40,000
Alban Lake	Paid	10,000
Flame Tree Publishing	Pro	4,000
Odd Tales of Wonder	Token	Not

		defined
Eibon Vale Press	Token	4,000
Third Flatiron	Paid	3000
FIYAH	Paid	7000
Alien Pub Magazine	Token	2,000
Augur	Token	Not stated
Snow Leopard Publishing	Charitable	2,500
Mythic Mag	Paid	6,000
Unidentified Funny Objects	Paid	5,000
Fairytale Review	Not stated	8,000
Reshwity Publishing (anthology)	Token	10,000
The Overcast (podcast)	Paid	5,000
Spring Song Press	Paid	10,000
Country Dark	Paid	10,000
4RV Publishing	Royalties	Not stated
Æther & Ichor	Token	5000
AHF Magazine	Token	3000
Allegory	Paid	No limit
Alcyone	Token	10000
Altered Reality Magazine	Token	Not stated
Animal: A Beast of a Literary Magazine	Token	Not stated
Anotherealm	Paid	5000
Aphotic Realm	Token	5000
Asymmetry Fiction	Paid	3000
The Wyrd	Paid	5000
Writers of the Future Contest	Paid	Not stated
The Worlds of Science Fiction, Fantasy and Horror	Paid	5000 to 10000
The WiFiles	Not stated	5000

The Weird Reader	Token	4500
3 Lobed Mag	Paid	7000
Stupefying Stories	Paid	10000
Stinkwaves Magazine	Not stated	3000
The Star-Lit Path	Token	7500
Pixie Forest Publishing	Paid	Varies
Castrum Press	Not stated (novella and novel length)	Not stated
Ombak	Pro	4000
Polu Texni	Pro	Not stated
Shock Totem	Pro	5000
Three-Lobed Burning Eye	Paid	1000-7000
Sub-Q Magazine	Pro	1000-5000
Little Blue Marble	Paid	2000 (5000 for reprints
Hinnom Magazine	Paid	250 - 5000
Enchanted Conversation	Paid	700-2000
LampLight	Paid	7000
Zombie Pirate Publishing	Token	7500
Blood Bath Literary Zine	Paid	2,500
Galli Books	Paid	7500
Waylines	Paid	6000
Farstrider Magazine	Paid	Not stated
Crossed Genres	Paid	6000
Black Denim Lit	Unpaid	7500
Sorghum and Spear	Paid	2,000 - 7,500
Parsec Ink	Paid	5,000
AGNI Magazine	Paid	No limit
B Cubed Press	Paid	500-5,000
The Irreal Café	Paid	2,000
Copper Nickel	Paid	Not stated

Flash Fiction - <1000

Aether and Ichor	Paid	Up to 3,000 but flash fic preferred
Bewildering Stories	Unpaid	Up to 3,000 but flash fic preferred
The Colored Lens	Paid	Up to 10,000 but flash fic preferred
Local Nomad	Unpaid	1,000
Dark Fire Fiction	Unpaid	Up to 5,000 but flash fic preferred
Deadman's Tome	Paid	1,000 and higher
Fictional Pairings	Token	200-1,000
Leading Edge	Paid	1,000 and higher
Mirror Dance	Token	Up to 6,000 but flash fic preferred
Fiction War	Paid	1,000
Door is Ajar	Token	1,000
Storyland Literary Review	Unpaid	1,000
Syntax & Salt Magazine	Paid	Up to 3,500
Tell Tale Press	Paid	500-5,000

Publishers of Long Fantasy Fiction

As with publishers of short fiction, publishers of long fiction have their own rules and industry terms. Most are open to submissions from everyone, referred to as *unsolicited submissions*. A few require you to have a literary agent before you can submit, known as *solicited submissions*.

Each publisher offers different payments depending on their stature. Most in the list offer royalties. Generally, only the big hitters offer advances but remember with advances you don't earn any money until the cost of that advance has been covered.

From what I've read on their websites, none of the below ask you to contribute financially toward publication. My advice would be to avoid partnering up with a publisher that asks you for such a contribution. Smaller publishers will have a much smaller marketing budget compared to the bigger fish in the sea, which means you'd have to do more promotional work, something we'll come to soon.

Name	Payment	Unsolicited Submissions
Tor Forge	Industry standard and royalties	During specified periods
Harper Voyager	Industry standard and royalties	During specified periods

Orbit Books	Industry standard and royalties	No
Gollancz	Industry standard and royalties	During specified periods
Baen	Competitive	Yes
Penguin Random House	Industry standard and royalties	No
Angry Robot	Industry standard a and royalties	No
Azure Spider Publications	Royalties	Yes
Barking Rain Press	Royalties	Yes
Class Act Books	Royalties	Yes
Dancing Star Press	Royalties	Yes
Edge Science Fiction and Fantasy Books	Small advance and royalties	Yes
Eraserhead Press	Royalties	Yes
eTreasures Publishing	Royalties	Yes
Fablecroft Publishing	Advance and royalties	Yes
Freedom Forge Press	Royalties	Yes
Gypsy Shadow	Royalties	Yes
Mundania Press	Royalties	Yes
IFWG	Royalties	Yes
Dead Ink	Royalties	Yes
Ink Smith Publishing	Royalties	Yes
JournalStone	Royalties	Yes

Twilight Times Books	Small advance and royalties	Yes
St Martin's Press (MacMillan)	Industry standard and royalties	No
Reliquary Press	Royalties	Yes
Pink Narcissus Press	Small advance and royalties	Yes
Founders House Publishing	Royalties	Yes
Quirk Books	Royalties	Yes
DAW	Advance and royalties	Yes
Literary Wanderlust	Royalties	Yes
Kensington Books	Royalties	Yes
Mirror World Publishing	Royalties	Yes
Mocha Memoir Press	Royalties	Yes
Montag Press	Royalties	Yes
Muse It Up Publishing	Royalties	Yes
Parvus Press	Advance and royalties	Yes
Priestess and Hierophan	Royalties	Yes
Pyr	Not stated	No
Resurrection House	Advance and royalties	Yes
Silver Leaf Books	Royalties	Yes
Soul Fire Press	Royalties	Yes
4RV Publishing	Royalties	Yes
Amphorae Publishing Group	Not stated	Yes
Bitingduck Press	Royalties	Yes

Black Bed Sheet	Not stated	Yes
Candlemark & Gleam	Royalties	Yes
Cuil Press	Royalties	Yes
Divertir Publishing	Royalties	Yes
Elder Signs Press	Royalties	Yes
Falstaff Book	Royalties	Yes
Castrum Press	Royalties	Yes
Crystal Peake Publisher Ltd	Royalties	Yes
Loose Leaves Publishing	Royalties	Yes
Nexxis Fantasy	Royalties	Yes
Orbannin Books	Royalties	Yes

Cover Letters

The task of writing a cover letter can sometimes feel tougher than writing the actual story. Luckily, guidance is plentiful and having studied that guidance, I've put together a few examples for you to use.

At this early stage, it's important to highlight that cover letters differ depending on whether it's a short story, or a longer piece, such as a novel—submission requirements are more substantial for the latter.

For short stories, the best guidance I've encountered comes from Alex Shvartsman, well-respected editor and writer of sci-fi and fantasy. Check out his guidance in full here: https://alexshvartsman.com/2016/05/09/how-to-write-a-proper-short-story-cover-letter/

Here are some of the highlights:

- If you know the name of the editor, address the cover letter to them. For instance, 'Dear Mr Gamgee'. If in doubt, just use 'Dear Editors'.

- Keep it simple. The editor is about to read your story, you don't need to tell them the ins and outs of character and plot. Let them discover it themselves. And if you explain it badly, you may put them off reading it altogether.

- If it's not relevant, don't include it. If you've got a law degree, nice work, but what has it got to do with the story? If your story is a legal drama, then that's a different matter.
- List some of your most notable publishing accomplishments. If you don't have any, that's fine! As Shvartsman says: "Every editor I know loves discovering new talent and loves being the first to publish someone, or first to publish someone in a pro venue. No one is going to hold a lack of past credits against you."

So, the examples. This is a cover letter I used for a short story called *Noodlin'*, published by Kzine in May 2019.

Dear Editors,

I attach for your consideration 'Noodlin'', a fantasy story around 2,800 words in length.

My short fiction has featured in *Aphelion Webzine, Alien Pub Magazine* and *Far Horizons,* and non-fiction in *Authors Publish Magazine.*

I appreciate you taking the time to consider my submission.

All the very best,

Richie

If, for instance, I was sending this story to a few publishers (AKA a simultaneous submission), it's wise to tell them you're doing so. An example may look something like this:

Dear Editors,

I attach for your consideration 'Noodlin'', a fantasy story around 2,800 words in length.

My short fiction has featured in *Aphelion Webzine, Alien Pub Magazine* and *Far Horizons,* and non-fiction in *Authors Publish Magazine.*

I have submitted this story to other publishers. Should it be accepted elsewhere I will, of course, inform you without delay.

I appreciate you taking the time to consider my submission.

All the very best,

Richie

For the avoidance of doubt, the text should not be bold. I've merely done so for easier reference.

So that's the practice for short stories, what about novels?

Publishers may ask for a short summary of the novel in the cover letter. How short depends on the publisher—they may ask for detail, they may ask for a mere sentence.

A standard accompaniment to the cover letter is a synopsis—what your story is *about*, i.e. the premise, the point of it; the characters, their emotional journey and the conflicts they face; the intended market, and; where it aligns in that market, for instance, comparing it to *Lord of the Rings.* The length is generally limited by publishers to one page. Invest a good amount of time in your synopsis. Make every word count. Read it aloud. Refine it until you can't say it any better. The synopsis helps an editor form their impression of your story so try and make the best one you can.

Marketing Methods

Marketing is perhaps one of the trickiest parts of the writing process. We've just spent months writing a book, the last thing we want to do is slave away on the web trying to unlock the magic code of getting it noticed.

I've tried various things—paid ads, joining forums and groups, going out to events. There seems to be no golden rule. What works for some may not work for others. Certain things do prove more effective, though, and these more effective means centre on one thing: *making connections.*

The mailing list

The email list is the thing we're told to be constantly building and nurturing. According to literary marketer Tim Grahl, email subscribers engage the most with content and yield the highest results when it comes to selling books or getting blog hits. But building a list isn't all too easy. Think of your own experience browsing websites. How many times have you felt compelled to enter your email address into a mailing list box? For me, not very often.

Unless there's a good reason to do so.

What does a reader get out of subscribing to your email list, save for the odd email from you? As much as we'd love to know what you're up to, the reality is we don't have the time. So instead, tease the reader with an incentive—a free short story, a guide on a particular subject, even a full book. Something the reader wants. Something useful.

Once you have your incentive in place you want to promote it on your platform as much as possible. On your website—if you have one—place sign up forms on every page, making them stand out and easy for people to use. No need to ask for their names or any other information; email address alone is sufficient, though be sure to read up on the GDPR changes. Generally, you can make a sign-up form GDPR compliant by adding a checkbox that has to be ticked, though more may be necessary. The best guides I've found are on Mailchimp, and on there you can also build GDPR compliant sign up forms for free. On Facebook or Twitter, make use of pinned posts and cover photos. Images and videos help attract attention so utilise them well.

One thing you could seek to include on your site is a pop-up form. Admittedly, I find pop-ups annoying. If I'm reading something and a form pops up I race to the 'x' button in a state of outraged annoyance. However, they *do* work. Using MailChimp, I designed a pop-up form and more people sign up using that than by any other method.

While on the subject of Mailchimp, I couldn't recommend it more highly for managing your mailing lists. It's easy to use and it's free. Another benefit is you can create automated emails, so when someone signs up they get an immediate email delivering your giveaways and updating them on everything you do. You can make a free pop-up form too, and it supplies you lots of analytics if you're into all that.

Getting out there

This method isn't as easy as making a pop-up form on your computer. It requires guts and determination, but it's perhaps the most effective marketing method of all.

Going to writer's events such as conferences, workshops, seminars, lectures, book launches, poetry nights, or readings are great ways to engage with potential readers. You can introduce yourself, tell them about your stories, and importantly, ask others about their writing. In doing so you're making all important connections, so when you publish new content those individuals are looking out for it, and you're looking out for theirs too.

Think of things you can take with you to events like this, things that will make people remember you and look you up. A pen with your platforms printed on it? A USB stick with a copy of one of your stories? I've even heard of one person buying Kindles and loading them with their own stories and handing them out to publishers and agents.

In this age of technology, it's easy to get lost behind screens, but one of the best methods is the most tried and tested—getting out there in the real world and shaking hands.

Engaging with others

Linked to meeting people, engaging with the blogs and platforms of other writers is another fantastic way of opening eyes to your writing.

We writers invest a hell of a lot of time in our content, so when someone takes the time to engage with us, man are we grateful. Simply liking and commenting on someone's article or tweet is an effective way to make an all-important connection. So set aside time to read the work of others and then tell them what you liked about it. If there's a particular blogger you like, why not invite them to guest blog on your website, or see if you can write for them?

Social media

Tim Grahl is of the view that social media platforms can be misleading, and I tend to agree. When I first created a Twitter account for my writing I was surprised by the number of people who began following me. Every time I logged on I'd have four or five new followers, and that's a lot for me. But then the next day they'd vanish like Bilbo Baggins. The reason? Fellow writers interested merely in gaining a follow for a follow, only then to unfollow you to seemingly boost their standing.

I'm reluctant to follow others back just because they followed me. They've made no effort to connect with me or my content. They're merely hunting the statistics, the follower count. When these individuals with their many thousands of followers come to promoting their work or content, their posts receive little interactions and nobody buys a thing. Why? All those followers aren't proper fans. No connections have been made.

Twitter is just one example. Facebook I've had more success with, but only to help promote content I've published. It cannot be relied upon, and the same goes for all social media platforms. Don't spend too much time on them!

About Richie Billing

I'm from a city called Liverpool, a place known mostly for The Beatles and football, yet it's one with a rich history, some of it good, some of it bad, and as a result, it's a gold mine of inspiration. I seriously got into writing fiction in about 2015 and fell completely in love. Now it's a part of my daily routine. I get grumpy when I don't get time to write.

Fantasy has been the genre that has captured my attention most. The book I have the fondest memories of reading as a youngster was *The Hobbit*, and I grew up in the *Harry Potter* and *Lord of the Rings* age so imaginative stories were what I knew and loved. As you've seen in this book, I don't just write fantasy. If I get an idea and I think it would make for a good story, I'll write it, regardless of genre, though often I find myself yearning for the fantastical and the endless possibilities it brings.

I study the craft of writing as much as time allows, and over the years I've read book after book, stacks of articles, attended lectures, seminars, workshops, courses and more. Much of what I've learned I've shared on my blog, *The Writer's Toolshed*, and in June 2019 I released *A Fantasy Writers' Handbook*, a detailed guide to writing fiction, the fantasy genre, and the things a writer can do to build their platform, market their scribblings, and get their stories published. Some people say it's good. See for yourself on Goodreads and Amazon.

My debut novel, *Pariah's Lament*, which at the time of writing this (October 2019), is nearly edited and will be published by *Fiction Vortex* in Spring 2020. If you like an underdog's tale filled with intrigue, conflict, and a hearty dose of action, I think you'll like this. You can find out more on my website.

And if you'd like to keep in touch, or wanted to drop me an email with a question or comment, please pay a visit to www.richiebilling.com. I've got lots of helpful things on there, including a free ebook on the craft of writing and lists of publishers and book reviewers. If you join my mailing list you'll be the first to learn about updates and additions to those resources, new blog posts, news on nifty writing tools, and special offers and opportunities.

Thank you for reading,

Richie

A Small Request

You've made it to the very last page of the book and for that I'm sincerely grateful. I hope you didn't grit your teeth and force your way through it, but instead enjoyed my words and found them of use. If you did, I'd be in your debt if you would share your thoughts on Amazon and/or Goodreads. Even if it's just a line, or a single word, it makes a massive difference. Crucially, it gives me reassurance, plus a lot of joy, to know that you enjoyed the book, which for me makes it all worthwhile. Secondly, it sends a positive message to the world of readers that it's a book worth reading, and as you know, it's a competitive field out there.

From the furthest reaches of my heart, I thank you for taking a chance on this book.

Richie

CPSIA information can be obtained
at www.ICGtesting.com
Printed in the USA
LVHW081600080221
678723LV00011B/698

9 781097 781331